IN BETWEEN THE SHEETS

Ian McEwan has written two collections of short stories, *First Love, Last Rites* and *In Between the Sheets,* and seven novels, *The Cement Garden, The Comfort of Strangers, The Child in Time, The Innocent, Black Dogs, The Daydreamer* and *Enduring Love.* He has also written several film scripts, including *The Imitation Game, The Ploughman's Lunch, Sour Sweet, The Good Son* and *The Innocent.*

Ian McEwan

IN BETWEEN
THE SHEETS

VINTAGE

Published by Vintage 1997

2 4 6 8 10 9 7 5 3 1

Copyright © Ian McEwan 1978

First published in Great Britain by
Jonathan Cape Ltd, 1978

Vintage
Random House, 20 Vauxhall Bridge Road,
London SW1V 2SA

Random House Australia (Pty) Limited
20 Alfred Street, Milsons Point, Sydney
New South Wales 2061, Australia

Random House New Zealand Limited
18 Poland Road, Glenfield,
Auckland 10, New Zealand

Random House South Africa (Pty) Limited
Endulini, 5A Jubilee Road, Parktown 2193,
South Africa

Random House UK Limited Reg. No. 954009

A CIP catalogue record for this book
is available from the British Library

ISBN 0 09 975471 1

Papers used by Random House UK Ltd are natural,
recyclable products made from wood grown in sustain-
able forests. The manufacturing processes conform to the
environmental regulations of the country of origin

Printed and bound in Great Britain by
The Guernsey Press Co. Ltd., Guernsey, Channel Islands

Author photograph © Annalena McAfee

TO VIC SAGE

CONTENTS

ACKNOWLEDGMENTS

The author and publishers wish to thank the following for permission to reproduce copyright material: *The New Review* for 'Pornography', 'Reflections of a Kept Ape', 'To and Fro' and 'In Between the Sheets'; *Encounter* for 'Saturday, March 199–' (published as 'Without Blood'); *Harpers/Queen* for 'Sunday, March 199–'; *Bananas* for 'Dead As They Come'; *American Review* for 'Psychopolis'; and Mick Jagger, Keith Richard and Essex Music International for the song extracts on pp. 84 and 85.

Pornography

❧❧❧

O'Byrne walked through Soho market to his brother's shop in Brewer Street. A handful of customers leafing through the magazines and Harold watching them through pebble-thick lenses from his raised platform in the corner. Harold was barely five foot and wore built-up shoes. Before becoming his employee O'Byrne used to call him Little Runt. At Harold's elbow a miniature radio rasped details of race meetings for the afternoon. 'So,' said Harold with thin contempt, 'the prodigal brother ... ' His magnified eyes fluttered at every consonant. He looked past O'Byrne's shoulder. 'All the magazines are for sale, gentlemen.' The readers stirred uneasily like troubled dreamers. One replaced a magazine and walked quickly from the shop. 'Where d'you get to?' Harold said in a quieter voice. He stepped from the dais, put on his coat and glared up at O'Byrne, waiting for an answer. Little Runt. O'Byrne was ten years younger than his brother, detested him and his success but now, strangely, wanted his approbation. 'I had an appointment, didn't I,' he said quietly. 'I got the clap.' Harold was pleased. He reached up and punched O'Byrne's shoulder playfully. 'Serves you,' he said and cackled theatrically. Another customer edged out of the shop. From the doorway Harold called, 'I'll be back at five.' O'Byrne smiled as his brother left. He hooked his thumbs into his jeans and sauntered towards the tight knot of customers. 'Can I help you gentlemen, the magazines are all for sale.' They scattered before him like frightened fowl, and suddenly he was alone in the shop.

A plump woman of fifty or more stood in front of a plastic shower curtain, naked but for panties and gasmask. Her hands hung limply at her sides and in one of them a cigarette smouldered. Wife of the Month. Since gasmasks and a thick rubber sheet on the bed, wrote JN of Andover, we've never looked back. O'Byrne played with the radio for a while then switched it off. Rhythmically he turned the pages of the magazine, and stopped to read the letters. An uncircumcised male virgin, without hygiene, forty-two next May, dared not peel back his foreskin now for fear of what he might see. I get these nightmares of worms. O'Byrne laughed and crossed his legs. He replaced the magazine, returned to the radio, switched it on and off rapidly and caught the unintelligible middle of a word. He walked about the shop straightening the magazines in the racks. He stood by the door and stared at the wet street intersected by the coloured strips of the plastic walk-thro. He whistled over and over a tune whose end immediately suggested its beginning. Then he returned to Harold's raised platform and made two telephone calls, both to the hospital, the first to Lucy. But Sister Drew was busy in the ward and could not come to the phone. O'Byrne left a message that he would not be able to see her that evening after all and would phone again tomorrow. He dialled the hospital switchboard and this time asked for trainee Nurse Shepherd in the children's ward. 'Hi,' O'Byrne said when Pauline picked up the phone. 'It's me.' And he stretched and leaned against the wall. Pauline was a silent girl who once wept in a film about the effects of pesticides on butterflies, who wanted to redeem O'Byrne with her love. Now she laughed, 'I've been phoning you all morning,' she said. 'Didn't your brother tell you?'

'Listen,' said O'Byrne, 'I'll be at your place about eight,' and replaced the receiver.

Harold did not return till after six, and O'Byrne was almost asleep, his head pillowed on his forearm. There were no customers. O'Byrne's only sale was *American Bitch*. 'Those American mags,' said Harold as he emptied the till of £15 and a handful of silver, 'are *good*.' Harold's new leather jacket. O'Byrne fingered it appreciatively. 'Seventy-eight quid,' said Harold and braced himself in front of the fish-eye mirror. His glasses flashed. 'It's all right,' said O'Byrne. 'Fucking right it is,' said Harold, and began to close up shop. 'Never take much on Wednesdays,' he said wistfully as he reached up and switched on the burglar alarm. 'Wednesday's a cunt of a day.' Now O'Byrne was in front of the mirror, examining a small trail of acne that led from the corner of his mouth. 'You're not fucking kidding,' he agreed.

Harold's house lay at the foot of the Post Office Tower and O'Byrne rented a room from him. They walked along together without speaking. From time to time Harold glanced sideways into a dark shop window to catch the reflection of himself and his new leather jacket. Little Runt. O'Byrne said, 'Cold, innit?' and Harold said nothing. Minutes later, when they were passing a pub, Harold steered O'Byrne into the dank, deserted public saying, 'Since you got the clap I'll buy you a drink.' The publican heard the remark and regarded O'Byrne with interest. They drank three scotches apiece, and as O'Byrne was paying for the fourth round Harold said, 'Oh yeah, one of those two nurses you've been knocking around with phoned.' O'Byrne nodded and wiped his lips. After a pause Harold said, 'You're well in there ... ' O'Byrne nodded again. 'Yep.' Harold's jacket shone. When he reached for his drink it creaked. O'Byrne was not going to tell him anything. He banged his hands together. 'Yep,' he said once more, and stared over his brother's head at the empty bar. Harold tried again. 'She wanted to know where you'd been ... ' 'I bet she did,' O'Byrne muttered, and then smiled.

Pauline, short and untalkative, her face bloodlessly pale, intersected by a heavy black fringe, her eyes large, green and watchful, her flat small, damp and shared with a secretary who was never there. O'Byrne arrived after ten, a little drunk and in need of a bath to purge the faint purulent scent that lately had hung about his fingers. She sat on a small wooden stool to watch him luxuriate. Once she leaned forwards and touched his body where it broke the surface. O'Byrne's eyes were closed, his hands floating at his side, the only sound the diminishing hiss of the cistern. Pauline rose quietly to bring a clean white towel from her bedroom, and O'Byrne did not hear her leave or return. She sat down again and ruffled, as far as it was possible, O'Byrne's damp, matted hair. 'The food is ruined,' she said without accusation. Beads of perspiration collected in the corners of O'Byrne's eyes and rolled down the line of his nose like tears. Pauline rested her hand on O'Byrne's knee where it jutted through the grey water. Steam turned to water on the cold walls, senseless minutes passed. 'Never mind, love,' said O'Byrne, and stood up.

Pauline went out to buy beer and pizzas, and O'Byrne lay down in her tiny bedroom to wait. Ten minutes passed. He dressed after cursory examination of his clean but swelling meatus, and wandered listlessly about the sitting room. Nothing interested him in Pauline's small collection of books. There were no magazines. He entered the kitchen in search of a drink. There was nothing but an overcooked meat pie. He picked round the burnt bits and as he ate turned the pages of a picture calendar. When he finished he remembered again he was waiting for Pauline. He looked at his watch. She had been gone now almost half an hour. He stood up quickly, tipping the kitchen chair behind him to the floor. He paused in the sitting room and then walked decisively out of the flat and slammed the front door on his way. He hurried down the stairs, anxious not to meet her now he had decided to get out. But she was there. Halfway up the second flight, a little out of breath, her arms full of bottles and tinfoil parcels. 'Where d'you get to?' said O'Byrne. Pauline stopped several steps down from him, her face tilted up awkwardly over her goods, the whites of her eyes and the tinfoil vivid in the dark. 'The usual place was closed. I had to walk miles . . . sorry.' They stood. O'Byrne was not hungry. He wanted to go. He hitched his thumbs into the waist of his jeans and cocked his head towards the invisible ceiling, then he looked down at Pauline who waited. 'Well,' he said at last, 'I was thinking of going.' Pauline came up, and as she pushed past whispered, 'Silly.' O'Byrne turned and followed her, obscurely cheated.

He leaned in the doorway, she righted the chair. With a movement of his head O'Byrne indicated that he wanted none of the food Pauline was setting out on plates. She poured him a beer and knelt to gather a few black pastry droppings from the floor. They sat in the sitting room. O'Byrne drank, Pauline ate slowly, neither spoke. O'Byrne finished all the beer and placed his hand on Pauline's knee. She did not turn. He said cheerily, 'What's wrong with you?' and she said, 'Nothing.' Alive with irritation O'Byrne moved closer and placed his arm protectively across her shoulders. 'Tell you what,' he half whispered. 'Let's go to bed.' Suddenly Pauline rose and went into the bedroom. O'Byrne sat with his hands clasped behind his head. He listened to Pauline undress, and he heard the creak of the bed. He got to his feet and, still without desire, entered the bedroom.

Pauline lay on her back and O'Byrne, having undressed quickly, lay beside her. She did not acknowledge him in her usual way, she did not move. O'Byrne raised his arm to stroke her shoulder, but instead let his hand fall back heavily against the sheet. They both lay on their backs in mounting silence, until O'Byrne decided to give her one last chance and with naked grunts hauled himself on to his elbow and arranged his face over hers. Her eyes, thick with tears, stared past him. 'What's the matter?' he said in resignatory sing-song. The eyes budged a fraction and fixed on his own. 'You,' she said simply. O'Byrne returned to his side of the bed, and after a moment said threateningly. 'I see.' Then he was up, and on top of her, and then past her and on the far side of the room. 'All right then ... ' he said. He wrenched his laces into a knot, and searched for his shirt. Pauline's back was to him. But as he crossed the sitting room her rising, accelerating wail of denial made him stop and turn. All white, in a cotton nightdress, she was there in the bedroom doorway and in the air, simultaneously at every point of arc in the intervening space, like the trick photographer's diver, she was on the far side of the room and she was at his lapels, knuckles in her mouth and shaking her head. O'Byrne smiled, and put his arms around her shoulders. Forgiveness swept through him. Clinging to each other they returned to the bedroom. O'Byrne undressed and they lay down again, O'Byrne on his back, Pauline with her head pillowed on his shoulder.

O'Byrne said, 'I never know what's going on in your mind,' and deeply comforted by this thought, he fell asleep. Half an hour later he woke. Pauline, exhausted by a week of twelve-hour shifts, slept deeply on his arm. He shook her gently. 'Hey,' he said. He shook her firmly, and as the rhythm of her breathing broke and she began to stir, he said in a laconic parody of some unremembered film, 'Hey, there's something we ain't done yet ... '

Harold was excited. When O'Byrne walked into the shop towards noon the following day Harold took hold of his arms and waved in the air a sheet of paper. He was almost shouting. 'I've worked it all out. I know what I want to do with the shop.' 'Oh yeah,' said O'Byrne dully, and put his fingers in his eyes and scratched till the intolerable itch there became a bearable pain. Harold rubbed his small pink hands together and explained rapidly. 'I'm going All American. I spoke to their rep on the phone this morning and he'll be here in half an hour. I'm getting rid of all the quid a time piss-in-her-cunt letters. I'm gonna carry the whole of the House of Florence range at £4·50 a time.'

O'Byrne walked across the shop to where Harold's jacket was spread across a chair. He tried it on. It was of course too small. 'And I'm going to call it Transatlantic Books,' Harold was saying. O'Byrne tossed the jacket on to the chair. It slid to the floor and deflated there like some reptilian air sac. Harold picked it up, and did not cease talking. 'If I carry Florence exclusive I get a special discount *and*,' he giggled, 'they pay for the fucking neon sign.'

O'Byrne sat down and interrupted his brother. 'How many of those soddin' inflatable women did you unload? There's still twenty-five of the fuckers in the cellar.' But Harold was pouring out scotch into two glasses. 'He'll be here in half an hour,' he repeated, and offered one glass to O'Byrne. 'Big deal,' said O'Byrne, and sipped. 'I want you to take the van over to Norbury and collect the order this afternoon. I want to get into this straight away.'

O'Byrne sat moodily with his drink while his brother whistled and was busy about the shop. A man came in and bought a magazine. 'See,' said O'Byrne sourly while the customer was still lingering over the tentacled condoms, 'he bought English, didn't he?' The man turned guiltily and left. Harold came and crouched by O'Byrne's chair and spoke as one who explains copulation to an infant. 'And what do I make? Forty per cent of 75p. Thirty p. Thirty fucking p. On House of Florence I'll make fifty per cent of £4·50. And that,' he rested his hand briefly on O'Byrne's knee, 'is what I call business.'

O'Byrne wriggled his empty glass in front of Harold's face, and waited patiently for his brother to fill it ... Little Runt.

The House of Florence warehouse was a disused church in a narrow terraced street on the Brixton side of Norbury. O'Byrne entered by the main porch. A crude plasterboard office and waiting room had been set up in the west end. The font was a large ash-tray in the waiting room. An elderly woman with a blue rinse sat alone in the office typing. When O'Byrne tapped on the sliding window she ignored him, then she rose and slid aside the glass panel. She took the order form he pushed towards her, glancing at him with unconcealed distaste. She spoke primly. 'You better wait there.' O'Byrne tap-danced abstractedly about the font, and combed his hair, and whistled the tune that went in a circle. Suddenly a shrivelled man with a brown coat and clipboard was at his side. 'Transatlantic Books?' he said. O'Byrne shrugged and followed him. They moved together slowly down long aisles of bolted steel shelves, the old man pushing a large trolley and O'Byrne walking a little in front with his hands clasped behind his back. Every few yards the warehouseman stopped, and with bad-tempered gasps lifted a thick pile of magazines from the shelves. The load on the trolley grew. The old man's breath echoed hoarsely around the church. At the end of the first aisle he sat down on the trolley, between his neat piles, and coughed and hawked for a minute or so into a paper handkerchief. Then, carefully folding the tissue and its ponderous green contents back into his pocket, he said to O'Byrne. 'Here, you're young. You push this thing.' And O'Byrne said, 'Push the fucker yourself. It's your job,' and offered the man a cigarette and lit it for him.

O'Byrne nodded at the shelves. 'You get some reading done here.' The old man exhaled irritably. 'It's all rubbish. It ought to be banned.' They moved on. At the end, as he was signing the invoice, O'Byrne said, 'Who you got lined up for tonight? Madam in the office there?' The warehouseman was pleased. His cackles rang out like bells, then tailed into another coughing fit. He leaned feebly against the wall, and when he had recovered sufficiently he raised his head and meaningfully winked his watery eye. But O'Byrne had turned and was wheeling the magazines out to the van.

Lucy was ten years older than Pauline, and a little plump. But her flat was large and comfortable. She was a sister and Pauline no more than a trainee nurse. They knew nothing of each other. At the underground station O'Byrne bought flowers for Lucy, and when she opened the door to him he presented them with a mock bow and the clicking of heels. 'A peace offering?' she said contemptuously and took the daffodils away. She had led him into the bedroom. They sat down side by side on the bed. O'Byrne ran his hand up her leg in a perfunctory kind of way. She pushed away his arm and said, 'Come on then. Where have you been the past three days?' O'Byrne could barely remember. Two nights with Pauline, one night in the pub with friends of his brother.

He stretched back luxuriously on the pink candlewick. 'You know ... working late for Harold. Changing the shop around. That kind of thing.'

'Those dirty books,' said Lucy with a little high-pitched laugh.

O'Byrne stood up and kicked off his shoes. 'Don't start that,' he said, glad to be off the defensive. Lucy leaned forwards and gathered up his shoes. 'You're going to ruin the backs of these,' she said busily, 'kicking them off like that.'

They both undressed. Lucy hung her clothes neatly in the wardrobe. When O'Byrne stood almost naked before her she wrinkled her nose in disgust. 'Is that you smelling?' O'Byrne was hurt. 'I'll have a bath,' he offered curtly.

Lucy stirred the bathwater with her hand, and spoke loudly over the thunder of the taps. 'You should have brought me some clothes to wash.' She hooked her fingers into the elastic of his pants. 'Give me these now and they'll be dry by the morning.' O'Byrne laced his fingers into hers in a decoy of affection. 'No, no,' he shouted rapidly. 'They were clean on this morning, they were.' Playfully Lucy tried to get them off. They wrestled across the bathroom floor, Lucy shrieking with laughter, O'Byrne excited but determined.

Finally Lucy put on her dressing gown and went away. O'Byrne heard her in the kitchen. He sat in the bath and washed away the bright green stains. When Lucy returned his pants were drying on the radiator. 'Women's Lib, innit?' said O'Byrne from the bath. Lucy said, 'I'm getting in too,' and took off her dressing gown. O'Byrne made room for her. 'Please yourself,' he said with a smile as she settled herself in the grey water.

O'Byrne lay on his back on the clean white sheets, and Lucy eased herself on to his belly like a vast nesting bird. She would have it no other way, from the beginning she had said, 'I'm in charge.' O'Byrne had replied, 'We'll see about that.' He was horrified, sickened, that he could enjoy being overwhelmed, like one of those cripples in his brother's magazines. Lucy had spoken briskly, the kind of voice she used for difficult patients. 'If you don't like it then don't come back.' Imperceptibly O'Byrne was initiated into Lucy's wants. It was not simply that she wished to squat on him. She did not want him to move. 'If you move again,' she warned him once, 'you've had it.' From mere habit O'Byrne thrust upwards and deeper, and quick as the tongue of a snake she lashed his face several times with her open palm. On the instant she came, and afterwards lay across the bed, half sobbing, half laughing. O'Byrne, one side of his face swollen and pink, departed sulking. You're a bloody pervert,' he had shouted from the door.

Next day he was back, and Lucy agreed not to hit him again. Instead she abused him. 'You pathetic helpless little shit,' she would scream at the peak of her excitement. And she seemed to intuit O'Byrne's guilty thrill of pleasure, and wish to push it further. One time she had suddenly lifted herself clear of him and, with a far-away smile, urinated on his head and chest. O'Byrne had struggled to get clear, but Lucy held him down and seemed deeply satisfied by his unsought orgasm. This time O'Byrne left the flat enraged. Lucy's strong, chemical smell was with him for days, and it was during this time that he met Pauline. But within the week he was back at Lucy's to collect, so he insisted, his razor, and Lucy was persuading him to try on her underwear. O'Byrne resisted with horror and excitement. 'The trouble with you,' said Lucy, 'is that you're scared of what you like.'

Now Lucy gripped his throat in one hand. 'You dare move,' she hissed, and closed her eyes. O'Byrne lay still. Above him Lucy swayed like a giant tree. Her lips were forming a word, but there was no sound. Many minutes later she opened her eyes and stared down, frowning a little as though struggling to place him. And all the while

she eased backwards and forwards. Finally she spoke, more
to herself than to him. 'Worm ... ' O'Byrne moaned.
Lucy's legs and thighs tightened and trembled. 'Worm ...
worm ... you little worm. I'm going to tread on you ...
dirty little worm.' Once more her hand was closed about
his throat. His eyes were sunk deep, and his word travelled
a long way before it left his lips. 'Yes,' he whispered.

The following day O'Byrne attended the clinic. The doc-
tor and his male assistant were matter-of-fact, unimpressed.
The assistant filled out a form and wanted details of
O'Byrne's recent sexual history. O'Byrne invented a
whore at Ipswich bus station. For many days after that he
kept to himself. Attending the clinic mornings and evenings, for injections, he was sapped of desire. When
Pauline or Lucy phoned, Harold told them he did not
know where O'Byrne was. 'Probably taken off for somewhere,' he said, winking across the shop at his brother.
Both women phoned each day for three or four days, and
then suddenly there were no calls from either.
   O'Byrne paid no attention. The shop was taking good
money now. In the evenings he drank with his brother and
his brother's friends. He felt himself to be both busy and
ill. Ten days passed. With the extra cash Harold was
giving him, he bought a leather jacket, like Harold's, but
somehow better, sharper, lined with red imitation silk. It
both shone and creaked. He spent many minutes in front
of the fish-eye mirror, standing sideways on, admiring the
manner in which his shoulders and biceps pulled the
leather to a tight sheen. He wore his jacket between the
shop and the clinic and sensed the glances of women in
the street. He thought of Pauline and Lucy. He passed a
day considering which to phone first. He chose Pauline,
and phoned her from the shop.
   Trainee Nurse Shepherd was not available, O'Byrne

was told after many minutes of waiting. She was sitting an examination. O'Byrne had his call transferred to the other side of the hospital. 'Hi,' he said when Lucy picked up the phone. 'It's me.' Lucy was delighted. 'When did you get back? Where have you been? When are you coming round?' He sat down. 'How about tonight?' he said. Lucy whispered in sex-kitten French, 'I can 'ardly wait ... ' O'Byrne laughed and pressed his thumb and forefinger against his forehead and heard other distant voices on the line. He heard Lucy giving instructions. Then she spoke rapidly to him. 'I've got to go. They've just brought a case in. About eight tonight then ... ' and she was gone.

O'Byrne prepared his story, but Lucy did not ask him where he had been. She was too happy. She laughed when she opened the door to him, she hugged him and laughed again. She looked different. O'Byrne could not remember her so beautiful. Her hair was shorter and a deeper brown, her nails were pale orange, she wore a short black dress with orange dots. There were candles and wine glasses on the dining table, music on the record player. She stood back, her eyes bright, almost wild, and admired his leather jacket. She ran her hands up the red lining. She pressed herself against it. 'Very smooth,' she said. 'Reduced to sixty quid,' O'Byrne said proudly, and tried to kiss her. But she laughed again and pushed him into a chair. 'You wait there and I'll get something to drink.'

O'Byrne lay back. From the record player a man sang of love in a restaurant with clean white tablecloths. Lucy brought an icy bottle of white wine. She sat on the arm of his chair and they drank and talked. Lucy told him recent stories of the ward, of nurses who fell in and out of love, patients who recovered or died. As she spoke she undid the top buttons of his shirt and pushed her hand down to his belly. And when O'Byrne turned in his chair and reached up for her she pushed him away, leaned down and kissed him on the nose. 'Now now,' she said primly. O'Byrne exerted himself. He recounted anecdotes he had heard in the pub. Lucy laughed crazily at the end of each, and as he was beginning the third she let her hand drop lightly between his legs and rest there. O'Byrne closed his eyes. The hand was gone and Lucy was nudging him. 'Go on,' she said. 'It was getting interesting.' He caught her wrist and wanted to pull her on to his lap. With a little sigh she slipped away and returned with a second bottle. 'We should have wine more often,' she said, 'if it makes you tell such funny stories.'

Encouraged, O'Byrne told his story, something about a car and what a garage mechanic said to a vicar. Once again Lucy was fishing round his fly and laughing, laughing. It was a funnier story than he thought. The floor rose and fell beneath his feet. And Lucy so beautiful, scented, warm ... her eyes glowed. He was paralysed by her teasing. He loved her, and she laughed and robbed him of his will. Now he saw, he had come to live with her, and each night she teased him to the edge of madness. He pressed his face into her breasts. 'I love you,' he mumbled, and again Lucy was laughing, shaking, wiping the tears from her eyes. 'Do you ... do you ... ' she kept trying to say. She emptied the bottle into his glass. 'Here's a toast ... ' 'Yeah,' said O'Byrne, 'To us.' Lucy was holding down her laughter. 'No, no,' she squealed. 'To *you*.' 'All right,' he said, and downed his wine in one. Then Lucy was standing in front of him pulling his arm. 'C'mon,' she said. 'C'mon.' O'Byrne struggled out of the chair. 'What about dinner then?' he said. 'You're the dinner,' she said, and they giggled as they tottered towards the bedroom.

As they undressed Lucy said, 'I've got a special little surprise for you so ... no fuss.' O'Byrne sat on the edge of

Lucy's large bed and shivered. 'I'm ready for anything,' he said. 'Good ... good,' and for the first time she kissed him deeply, and pushed him gently backwards on to the bed. She climbed forward and sat astride his chest. O'Byrne closed his eyes. Months ago he would have resisted furiously. Lucy lifted his left hand to her mouth and kissed each finger. 'Hmmm ... the first course.' O'Byrne laughed. The bed and the room undulated softly about him. Lucy was pushing his hand towards the top corner of the bed. O'Byrne heard a distant jingle, like bells. Lucy knelt by his shoulder, holding down his wrist, buckling it to a leather strap. She had always said she would tie him up one day and fuck him. She bent low over his face and they kissed again. She was licking his eyes and whispering, 'You're not going anywhere,' O'Byrne gasped for air. He could not move his face to smile. Now she was tugging at his right arm, pulling it, stretching it to the far corner of the bed. With a dread thrill of compliance O'Byrne felt his arm die. Now that was secure and Lucy was running her hands along the inside of his thigh, and on down to his feet ... he lay stretched almost to breaking, splitting, fixed to each corner, spread out against the white sheet. Lucy knelt at the apex of his legs. She stared down at him with a faint, objective smile, and fingered herself delicately. O'Byrne lay waiting for her to settle on him like a vast white nesting bird. She was tracing with the tip of one finger the curve of his excitement, and then with thumb and forefinger making a tight ring about its base. A sigh fled between his teeth. Lucy leaned forwards. Her eyes were wild. She whispered, 'We're going to get you, me and Pauline are ... '

Pauline. For an instant, syllables hollow of meaning. 'What?' said O'Byrne, and as he spoke the word he remembered, and understood a threat. 'Untie me,' he said quickly. But Lucy's finger curled under her crotch and her eyes half closed. Her breathing was slow and deep. 'Untie me,' he shouted, and struggled hopelessly with his straps. Lucy's breath came now in light little gasps. As he struggled, so they accelerated. She was saying something ... moaning something. What was she saying? He could not hear. 'Lucy,' he said, 'please untie me.' Suddenly she was silent, her eyes wide open and clear. She climbed off the bed. 'Your friend Pauline will be here, soon,' she said, and began to get dressed. She was different, her movements brisk and efficient, she no longer looked at him. O'Byrne tried to sound casual. His voice was a little high. 'What's going on?' Lucy stood at the foot of the bed buttoning her dress. Her lip curled. 'You're a bastard,' she said. The doorbell rang and she smiled. 'Now that's good timing, isn't it?'

'Yes, he went down very quietly,' Lucy was saying as she showed Pauline into the bedroom. Pauline said nothing. She avoided looking at either O'Byrne or Lucy. And O'Byrne's eyes were fixed on the object she carried in her arms. It was large and silver, like an outsized electric toaster. 'It can plug in just here,' said Lucy. Pauline set it down on the bedside table. Lucy sat down at her dressing table and began to comb her hair. 'I'll get some water for it in a minute,' she said.

Pauline went and stood by the window. There was silence. Then O'Byrne said hoarsely, 'What's that thing?' Lucy turned in her seat. 'It's a steriliser,' she said breezily. 'Steriliser?' 'You know, for sterilising surgical instruments.' The next question O'Byrne did not dare ask. He felt sick and dizzy. Lucy left the room. Pauline continued to stare out the window into the dark. O'Byrne felt the need to whisper. 'Hey, Pauline, what's going on?' She turned to face him, and said nothing. O'Byrne discovered that the strap round his right wrist was slackening a little, the leather was stretching. His hand was concealed by pillows. He worked it backwards and forwards, and spoke urgently. 'Look, let's get out of here. Undo these things.'

For a moment she hesitated, then she walked round the side of the bed and stared down at him. She shook her head. 'We're going to get you.' The repetition terrified him. He thrashed from side to side. 'It's not my idea of a fucking joke,' he shouted. Pauline turned away. 'I hate you,' he heard her say. The right-hand strap gave a little more. 'I hate you. I hate you.' He pulled till he thought his arm would break. His hand was too large still for the noose around his wrist. He gave up.

Now Lucy was at the bedside pouring water into the steriliser. 'This is a sick joke,' said O'Byrne. Lucy lifted a flat, black case on to the table. She snapped it open and began to take out long-handled scissors, scalpels and other bright, tapering, silver objects. She lowered them carefully into the water. O'Byrne started to work his right hand again. Lucy removed the black case and set on the table two white kidney bowls with blue rims. In one lay two hypodermic needles, one large, one small. In the other was cotton wool. O'Byrne's voice shook. 'What is all this?' Lucy rested her cool hand on his forehead. She enunciated with precision. 'This is what they should have done for you at the clinic.' 'The clinic ... ?' he echoed. He could see now that Pauline was leaning against the wall drinking from a bottle of scotch. 'Yes,' said Lucy, reaching down to take his pulse. 'Stop you spreading round your secret little diseases.' 'And telling lies,' said Pauline, her voice strained with indignation.

O'Byrne laughed uncontrollably. 'Telling lies ... telling lies,' he spluttered. Lucy took the scotch from Pauline and raised it to her lips. O'Byrne recovered. His legs were shaking. 'You're both out of your minds.' Lucy tapped the steriliser and said to Pauline, 'This will take a few minutes yet. We'll scrub down in the kitchen.' O'Byrne tried to raise his head. 'Where are you going?' he called after them. 'Pauline ... Pauline.'

But Pauline had nothing more to say. Lucy stopped in the bedroom doorway and smiled at him. 'We'll leave you a pretty little stump to remember us by,' and she closed the door.

On the bedside table the steriliser began to hiss. Shortly after it gave out the low rumble of boiling water, and inside the instruments clinked together gently. In terror he pumped his hand. The leather was flaying the skin off his wrist. The noose was riding now round the base of his thumb. Timeless minutes passed. He whimpered and pulled, and the edge of the leather cut deep into his hand. He was almost free.

The door opened, and Lucy and Pauline carried in a small, low table. Through his fear O'Byrne felt excitement once more, horrified excitement. They arranged the table close to the bed. Lucy bent low over his erection. 'Oh dear ... oh dear,' she murmured. With tongs Pauline lifted instruments from the boiling water and laid them out in neat silver rows on the starched white tablecloth she had spread across the table. The leather noose slipped forwards fractionally. Lucy sat on the edge of the bed and took the large hypodermic from the bowl. 'This will make you a little sleepy,' she promised. She held it upright and expelled a small jet of liquid. And as she reached for the cotton wool O'Byrne's arm pulled clear. Lucy smiled. She set aside the hypodermic. She leaned forwards once more ... warm, scented ... she was fixing him with wild red eyes ... her fingers played over his tip ... she held him still between her fingers. 'Lie back, Michael, my sweet.' She nodded briskly at Pauline. 'If you'll secure that strap, Nurse Shepherd, then I think we can begin.'

Reflections of a Kept Ape

❖❖❖

Eaters of asparagus know the scent it lends the urine. It has been described as reptilian, or as a repulsive inorganic stench, or again as a sharp, womanly odour ... exciting. Certainly it suggests sexual activity of some kind between exotic creatures, perhaps from a distant land, another planet. This unworldly smell is a matter for poets and I challenge them to face their responsibilities. All this ... a preamble that you may discover me as the curtain rises, standing, urinating, reflecting in a small overheated closet which adjoins the kitchen. The three walls which fill my vision are painted a bright and cloying red, decorated by Sally Klee when she cared for such things, a time of remote and singular optimism. The meal, which passed in total silence and from which I have just risen, consisted of a variety of tinned foods, compressed meat, potatoes, asparagus, served at room temperature. It was Sally Klee who opened the tins and set their contents on paper plates. Now I linger at my toilet washing my hands, climbing on to the sink to regard my face in the mirror, yawning. Do I deserve to be ignored?

I find Sally Klee as I left her. She is in her dining room playing with used matches in a musty pool of light. We were lovers once, living almost as man and wife, happier than most wives and men. Then she wearying of my ways and I daily exacerbating her displeasure with my persistence, we now inhabit different rooms. Sally Klee does not look up as I enter the room, and I hover between her chair and mine, the plates and tins arranged before me. Perhaps I am a little too squat to be taken seriously, my arms a little too long. With them I reach out and stroke gently Sally Klee's gleaming black hair. I feel the warmth of her skull beneath her hair and it touches me, so alive, so sad.

Perhaps you will have heard of Sally Klee. Two and a half years ago she published a short novel and it was an instant success. The novel describes the attempts and bitter failures of a young woman to have a baby. Medically there appears to be nothing wrong with her, nor with her husband, nor his brother. In the words of *The Times Literary Supplement*, it is a tale told with 'wan deliberation'. Other serious reviews were less kind, but in its first year it sold thirty thousand copies in hardback, and so far a quarter of a million in paperback. If you have not read the book you will have seen the cover of the paperback edition as you buy your morning paper at the railway station. A naked woman kneels, face buried in hands, amidst a barren desert. Since that time Sally Klee has written nothing. Every day for months on end she sits at her typewriter, waiting. But for a sudden flurry of activity at the end of each day her machine is silent. She cannot remember how she wrote her first book, she does not dare depart from what she knows, she does not dare repeat herself. She has money and time and a comfortable house in which she languishes, bored and perplexed, waiting.

Sally Klee places her hand on mine as it moves across her head, either to forestall or acknowledge tenderness — her head is still bowed and I cannot see her face. Knowing nothing, I compromise and hold her hand and seconds later our hands drop limply to our sides. I say nothing and, like the perfect friend, begin to clear away the plates and

cutlery, tins and tin opener. In order to assure Sally Klee
that I am not at all piqued by or sulking at her silence I
whistle Lillibulero cheerfully through my teeth, rather in
the manner of Sterne's Uncle Toby in times of stress.

Exactly so. I am stacking the plates in the kitchen and
sulking, almost to the point of forgetting to whistle.
Despite my negative sentiments I set about preparing the
coffee. Sally Klee will have a blend of no less than four
different kinds of bean in emulation of Balzac whose life
she read in a lavishly illustrated volume while attending
to the proofs of her first novel. We always call it her *first*
novel. The beans must be measured out carefully and
ground by hand – a task to which my physique is well
suited. Secretly, I suspect, Sally Klee believes that good
coffee is the essence of authorship. Look at Balzac (I
believe she says to herself), who wrote several thousand
novels and whose coffee bills present themselves to the
well-wisher from behind glass cases in tranquil suburban
museums. After the grinding I must add a little salt and
pour the mixture into the silver cavity of a compact,
stainless-steel machine sent here by post from Grenoble.
While this warms on the stove I peer in at Sally Klee
from behind the dining-room door. She has folded her
arms now and is resting them on the table in front of her.
I advance a few paces into the room, hoping to catch her
eye.

Perhaps from the very beginning the arrangement was
certain to fail. On the other hand, the pleasures it afforded
– particularly to Sally Klee – were remarkable. And while
she believes that in my behaviour towards her I was a
little too persistent, too manic, too 'eager', and while I for
my part still feel she delighted more in my unfamiliarity
('funny little black leathery penis' and 'your saliva tastes
like weak tea') than in my essential self, I would like to
think there are no profound regrets on either side. As

Moira Sillito, the heroine of Sally Klee's first novel, says to herself at her husband's funeral, 'Everything changes.' Is the quiet, assertive yet ultimately tragic Moira consciously misquoting Yeats? So, no lasting regrets, I hope, when, this afternoon, I carried my few personal effects from Sally Klee's spacious bedroom to my own small room at the top of the house. Yes, I rather like to climb stairs, and I left without a murmur. In effect (why deny it?) I was dismissed, but I had my own reasons for quitting those sheets. This liaison, for all its delights, was involving me too deeply in Sally Klee's creative problems and only a final act of good-natured voyeurism could show me how far out of my depth I was. Artistic gestation is a private matter and my proximity was, and perhaps is still, obscene. Sally Klee's gaze lifts clear of the table and for an immeasurable moment meets my own. With a slight affirmative motion of the head she indicates she is ready to take coffee.

Sally Klee and I sip our coffee 'in pregnant silence'. This at least is how Moira and her husband Daniel, a rising young executive at a local bottling factory, sip their tea and digest the news that there are no medical reasons why between them they should be incapable of producing a child. Later the same day they decide to try (a good word, I thought) yet again for a baby. Personally speaking, sipping is something at which I rather excel, but silence, of whatever kind, makes me uncomfortable. I hold the cup several inches away from my face and propel my lips towards the rim in a winsome, tapering pout. Simultaneously I roll my eyes into my skull. There was a time — I remember the first occasion particularly — when the whole performance brought a smile to the less flexible lips of Sally Klee. Now I excel uncomfortably and when my eyeballs are facing outwards into the world once more I see no smile but Sally Klee's pale, hairless fingers drumming on the polished surface of the dining table. She refills her cup, stands and leaves the room, leaves me to listen to her footsteps on the stairs.

Though I remain below I am with her every inch of the way – I have said my proximity is obscene. She ascends the stairs, enters her bedroom, sits at her table. From where I sit I hear her thread into her typewriter a single sheet of paper, off-white, A4, 61 mg per square metre, the very same paper on which she effortlessly composed her first novel. She will ensure the machine is set at double space. Only letters to her friends, agent and publisher go at single space. Decisively she punches the red key which will provide, when there are words to surround it, a neat, off-white emptiness to precede her first sentence. An awesome silence settles over the house, I commence to writhe in my chair, an involuntary high-pitched sound escapes my throat. For two and a half years Sally Klee has grappled not with words and sentences, nor with ideas, but with form, or rather, with tactics. Should she, for instance, break silence with a short story, work a single idea with brittle elegance and total control? But what single idea, what sentence, what word? Moreover, good short stories are notoriously hard to write, harder perhaps than novels, and mediocre stories lie thick on the ground. Perhaps then another novel about Moira Sillito. Sally Klee closes her eyes and looks hard at her heroine and discovers yet again that everything she knows about her she has already written down. No, a second novel must break free of the first. What about a novel set (my tentative suggestion) in the jungles of South America? How ridiculous! What then? Moira Sillito stares up at Sally Klee from the empty page. Write about me, she says simply. But I can't, Sally Klee cries out loud, I know nothing more about you. Please, says Moira. Leave me alone, Sally Klee cries out louder than before. Me, me, says Moira. No, no, Sally Klee shouts, I know nothing, I hate you. Leave me alone!

Sally Klee's cries pierce many hours of tense silence and bring me to my feet trembling. When will I ever accustom myself to these terrible sounds which cause the very air to bend and warp with strain? In calmer retrospection I will be reminded of Edvard Munch's famous woodcut, but now I scamper about the dining room, unable to stifle the agitated squeals which well from me in moments of panic or excitement and which, to Sally Klee's ears, diminish my romantic credibility. And at night when Sally Klee shouts in her sleep, my own pathetic squeals render me dismally incapable of giving comfort. Moira has nightmares too, as is established with chilling economy in the first line of Sally Klee's first novel: 'That night pale Moira Sillito rose screaming from her bed ... ' *The Yorkshire Post* was one of the few papers to take notice of this opening but, sadly, found it 'too energetic by half'. Moira of course has a husband to soothe her and by the foot of page two she is 'sleeping like a little child in the young man's strong arms'. In a surprise review the feminist magazine *Refractory Girl* quotes this line to evidence the redundance of both 'little' and the novel's 'banal sexism'. However, I found the line poignant, more so when it describes the very solace I yearn to bring in the dead of night to its begetter.

I am silenced by the scrape of a chair. Sally Klee will come downstairs now, enter the kitchen to fill her cup with cold, black coffee and then return to her desk. I climb on to the chaise longue and arrange myself there in an attitude of simian preoccupation in case she should look in. Tonight she passes by, her form framed briefly in the open doorway, while her cup, rattling harshly in its saucer, announced her nervous wretchedness. Upstairs again I hear her remove the sheet of paper from her typewriter and replace it with a fresh piece. She sighs and presses the red key, pushes her hair clear of her eyes and begins to type at her steady, efficient forty words per minute. Music fills the house. I stretch my limbs on the chaise longue and drift into an after-dinner sleep.

I familiarised myself with Sally Klee's ritual ordeals during my brief residence in her bedroom. I lay on her bed, she sat at the desk, in our separate ways doing nothing. I luxuriated in, I congratulated myself hourly on, my recent elevation from pet to lover and, stretched out on my back, arms folded behind my head, legs crossed, I speculated upon further promotion, from lover to husband. Yes, I saw myself, expensive fountain pen in hand, signing hire purchase agreements for my pretty wife. I would teach myself to hold a pen. I would be man-about-the-house, scaling drainpipes with uxorious ease to investigate the roof gutters, suspending myself from light fittings to re-decorate the ceiling. Down to the pub in the evening with my husband credentials to make new friends, invent a name for myself in order to bestow it on my wife, take up wearing slippers about the house, and perhaps even socks and shoes outside. Of genetic rules and regulations I knew too little to reflect on the possibility of progeny, but I was determined to consult medical authorities who would in turn inform Sally Klee of her fate. She meanwhile sat before her empty page, pale as screaming, rising Moira Sillito, but silent and still, progressing ineluctably towards the crisis which would bring her to her feet and propel her downstairs for unwarmed coffee. In the early days she cast in my direction nervous encouraging smiles and we were happy. But as I came to know of the agony behind her silence my empathic squeals – so she was to insinuate – made it harder to concentrate and the smiles in my direction ceased.

They ceased and, therefore, likewise my speculations. I am not, as you may have gathered, one to seek confrontations. Think of me rather as one who would suck yolks from eggs without damage to the shells, remember my dextrous sipping. Beyond my silly noises, which were more evolutionary than personal, I said nothing. Late one evening, overwhelmed by a sudden intuition, I scampered into the bathroom minutes after Sally Klee had left it. I locked the door, stood on the edge of the bath, opened the small, scented cupboard in which she kept her most private, womanly things and confirmed what I already knew. Her intriguing cap still lay inside its plastic oyster, dusted and somehow disapproving of me. I passed rapidly then, in the long afternoons and evenings on the bed, from speculation to nostalgia. The long prelude of mutual exploration, she counting my teeth with her ballpoint pen, I searching in vain for nits in her copious hair. Her playful observations on the length, colour, texture of my member, my fascination with her endearingly useless toes and coyly concealed anus. Our first 'time' (Moira Sillito's word) was a little dogged by misunderstanding largely due to my assumption that we were to proceed *a posteriori*. That matter was soon resolved and we adopted Sally Klee's unique 'face to face', an arrangement I found at first, as I tried to convey to my lover, too fraught with communication, a little too 'intellectual'. However, I rapidly made myself comfortable, and not two afternoons later was bringing to mind:

> And pictures in our eyes to get
> Was all our propagation.

Fortunately it was not, at this stage, quite all. 'The experience of falling in love is common but nevertheless ineffable.' These sentiments are offered to Moira Sillito by her brother-in-law, the only one of a large family to have been to a university. I should add that Moira, though familiar with the word from the hymns of her schooldays, does not know what 'ineffable' means. After a suitable silence she excuses herself, runs upstairs to the bedroom, finds the word in a pocket dictionary there, runs downstairs to the living room and says cosily as she comes through the door, 'No, it is not. Falling in love is like floating on clouds.' Like Moira Sillito's brother-in-law, I was in love and, as will happen, it was not long before my tirelessness began to oppress Sally Klee, nor was it long before she complained that the friction of our bodies brought her out in a rash, and that my 'alien seed' (alien corn, I quipped fruitlessly at the time) was aggravating her thrush. This and my 'bloody gibbering on the bed' precipitated the end of the affair, the happiest eight days of my life. I will be two and a half next April.

After speculation, after nostalgia, and before my removal to the room upstairs, I had leisure to pose myself certain questions concerning Sally Klee's creative ordeals. Why, after a long day of inactivity before one blank sheet of paper, did she return to the room in the evening with her unwarmed coffee and replace that sheet with another? What was it she then began to type so fluently that each day took up only one sheet of paper and was afterwards filed with a thick bank of other such sheets? And why did this sudden activity not offer her relief from her quiet suffering, why did she rise from her table each night still pained, preoccupied with the emptiness of the other sheet? Certainly the sound of the keys was release for me, and invariably at the very first stroke I fell into a grateful sleep. Have I not left myself dozing in the crystalline present on the chaise longue downstairs? Once, instead of falling asleep I sidled up to Sally Klee's chair on the pretext of affection and glimpsed the words 'in which case the whole thing could be considered from' before my lover – as

she still was then — kissed me gently on the ear and shoved
me tenderly in the direction of the bed. This rather
pedestrian construction dulled my curiosity, but only for a
day or two. What whole thing? What whole thing could
be considered from what? A few days later the plastic
oyster had ceased to yield up its rubber pearl and I began
to feel that I, as Sally Klee's rejected lover, had the right
to know the contents of what I had come to regard as a
private diary. Between them curiosity and vanity con-
cocted a balm to ease my prying conscience, and like an
out-of-work actor I longed to see a favourable notice of
myself, even one relating — as it were — to a past produc-
tion.

While Sally Klee sat at her table I had lain in luxury,
planning her future and mine, I then had lain there in
remorse and now, as our incommunicativeness became
firmly established, I lay in wait. I stayed awake late into
the evening in order to watch her as she opened a drawer
in her desk, removed from it a faded, blue clasp file,
peeled from her typewriter the completed sheet, placed it
face downwards in the file to ensure (I surmised through
half closed eyes) that the earliest entries were on top,
closed the file and returned it to its drawer, closed the
drawer and stood, eyes dulled by exhaustion and defeat,
jaw slack, spirit oblivious to the lover-turned-spy feigning
sleep on her bed, making his silent calculations. Though
not remotely altruistic, my intentions were not purely
selfish either. Naturally I hoped that by gaining access to
Sally Klee's most intimate secrets and sorrows I might, by
pitting my strength against selected locales of her clan-
destine frailty, persuade her that itch, thrush and gibbering were small prices to pay for my boundless affection.
On the other hand I did not think only of myself. I ran
and re-ran fantasy footage which show me poring over the
journal while its author was out of the house, me confessing

to Sally Klee on her return my slight treachery and con-
gratulating her with passionate embrace before she can
draw breath on having written a masterpiece, a colossal
and devastating psychic journey, she sinking into the chair
I deftly proffer, eyes widening and glowing with the dawn-
ing realisation of the truth of what I say, us, shot here in
tight close-up, studying the journal long into the night,
me advising, guiding, editing, the publisher's rapturous
reception of the manuscript outdone by that of the critics
and that in turn by the reading, buying public, the
renewal of Sally Klee's writing confidence, the renewal,
through our co-operative endeavours, of our mutual
understanding and love ... yes, renewal, renewal, my film
was all about renewal.

It was not until today that an opportunity finally
offered itself. Sally Klee was obliged to visit her accountant
in town. In order to sublimate my near-hysterical excitement I performed kind services at high speed. While she
retired to the bathroom to arrange her hair before the
mirror there, I searched the house for bus and train timetables and pushed them under the bathroom door. I
climbed the hat tree and plucked from its highest branch
Sally Klee's red silk scarf and ran to her with it. After she
had left the house, however, I noticed the scarf back in its
position. Had I not offered it, I conjectured sulkily as I
watched her at the bus stop from the attic window, she
would most likely have worn it. Her bus was a long time
coming (she should have consulted the timetables) and I
watched her pace round the concrete post and finally
engage in conversation with a woman who also waited
and who carried a child on her back, a sight which com-
municated to me across the suburban gables a chemical
pang of generic longing. I was determined to wait until
I had seen the bus carry Sally Klee away. Like Moira
Sillito gazing, in the long days that followed her husband's

funeral, at a snapshot of his brother, I did not wish to appear, even to myself, precipitate. The bus came and the pavement was suddenly and conspicuously vacant. Touched by a momentary sense of loss I turned away from the window.

Sally Klee's desk is unpretentious, standard office equipment of the kind used by middle-stratum administrators of hospitals and zoos, its essential constituent being plywood. The design is simplicity itself. A plain writing surface rests on two parallel banks of drawers, and the whole is backed by one lacquered sheet of wood. I had long ago noted that the typed sheets were filed in the top left side drawer, and my initial reaction on descending from the attic and finding it locked was one of anger rather than despair. Was I not to be trusted then after so long an intimacy, was this how one species in its arrogance treated another? As an insult of omission, all the other drawers slid out like mocking tongues and displayed their dull stationery contents. In the face of this betrayal (what else had she locked? The fridge? The greenhouse?) of our shared past I felt my claim to the faded blue clasp file utterly vindicated. From the kitchen I fetched a screwdriver and with it set about prising loose the sheet of flimsy wood that bound the back of the desk. With a sound like the crack of a whip a large piece detached itself along a line of weakness, and left in its place an ugly rectangular hole. I was not concerned with appearances however. I thrust my hand deep inside, found the back of the drawer, insinuated my fingers farther, finding the file began to lift it clear and, had not its leading edge caught on a nail and tipped its contents in a white swarm on to the splinter-strewn floor, could have congratulated myself on an impeccable appropriation. Instead I gathered as many sheets as my left foot could convey to my right hand in one continuous movement, and retired to the bed.

I closed my eyes and, in the manner of those who, poised above the pan, fleetingly hug their faeces to their bowels, retained the moment. For the sake of future recollection, I concentrated on the precise nature of my expectations. I was well aware of the universal law which pre-ordains a discrepancy between the imagined and the real – I even prepared myself for a disappointment. When I opened my eyes a number filled my vision – 54. Page 54. Below that I found myself halfway through a sentence which had its origins on page fifty-three, a sentence sinister in its familiarity. 'said Dave, carefully wiping his lips with it and crumpling it on to his plate.' I turned my face into the pillow, sickened and stunned by an apprehension of the complexity and sophistication of Sally Klee's species and the brutish ignorance of my own. 'Dave stared intently through the candlelight at his sister-in-law and her husband, his brother. He spoke quietly. "Or again some think of it as a sharp, womanly odour (he glanced at Moira) ... exciting. Certainly it suggests sexual activity of some ... " ' I threw the sheet aside and clutched at another, page 196: 'of earth struck the coffin lid, the rain ceased as suddenly as it had begun. Moira detached herself from the main group and wandered across the cemetery, reading without real comprehension the inscriptions on the stones. She felt mellow, as if she had seen a depressing but ultimately good film. She stopped under a yew tree and stood there a long time, abstractedly picking at the bark with her long orange finger nails. She thought, Everything changes. A sparrow, its feathers fluffed against the cold, hopped forlornly at her feet.' Not one phrase, not one word modified, everything unaltered. Page 230: '-ing on clouds?" Dave repeated peevishly. "What exactly does that mean?" Moira let her gaze fall on a flaw in the Bokhara design and said nothing. Dave crossed the room and took her hand. "What I mean when I ask that," he said hurriedly, "is that I have so many things to learn from you. You've suffered so much. You know so much." Moira released her hand to pick up her cup of barely warm, weak tea. She thought listlessly, Why do men despise women?'

I could read no more. I squatted on the bed post picking at my chest, listening to the ponderous tick of the clock in the hallway downstairs. Was art then nothing more than a wish to appear busy? Was it nothing more than a fear of silence, of boredom, which the merely reiterative rattle of the typewriter's keys was enough to allay? In short, having crafted one novel, would it suffice to write it again, type it out with care, page by page? (Gloomily I recycled nits from torso to mouth.) Deep in my heart I knew it would suffice and, knowing that, seemed to know less than I had ever known before. Two and a half next April indeed! I could have been born the day before yesterday.

It was growing dark when I finally set about arranging the papers and returning them to the file. I worked quickly, turning pages with all four limbs, driven less by the fear of Sally Klee returning home early than by an obscure hope that by restoring order I could erase the afternoon from my mind. I eased the file through the back of the desk and into its drawer. I secured the jagged segment of wood with drawing pins hammered down with the heel of a shoe. I threw the splinters of wood out the window and pushed the desk against the wall. I crouched in the centre of the room, knuckles barely brushing the carpet, questioning the semi-darkness and the frightful hiss of total silence about my head ... now everything was as it had been and as Sally Klee would expect it to be – typewriter, pens, blotting paper, a single withering daffodil – and still I knew what I knew and understood nothing at all. Simply, I was unworthy. I did not wish to turn on the light and illuminate my memories of the happiest eight days of my life. I groped, therefore, in the gloom unique to bedrooms until, vibrant with self-pity, I had located all of my few possessions – hairbrush, nail file, stainless-steel mirror and toothpicks. My resolve to leave the room without once looking back failed me when I reached the bedroom door. I turned and peered, but I could see nothing. I closed the door softly behind me and, even as I set my hand on the first step of the narrow attic staircase, I heard Sally Klee's key scratching for leverage in the front door lock.

I wake from my after-dinner sleep into silence. Perhaps silence, the sudden cessation of Sally Klee's typewriter, has woken me. My empty coffee cup still hangs by its handle from my finger, a viscous residue of tinned foods coats my tongue, whereas a trickle of saliva from my sleeping mouth has stained the paisley pattern of the chaise longue. Sleep after all solves nothing. I rise scratching and long for my toothpicks (fishbone in chamois pouch) but now they are at the very top of the house and to fetch them I should have to pass Sally Klee's open door. And why should I not pass her open door? Why should I not be seen and be taken account of in this household? Am I invisible? Do I not deserve for my quiet, self-effacing removal to another room a simple acknowledgment, the curt exchange of nods and sighs and smiles between two who have known both suffering and loss? I find myself standing before the hallway clock, watching the small hand edge toward ten. The truth is that I do not pass her door because I smart from being ignored, because I *am* invisible and of no account. Because I long to pass her door. My eyes stray to the front door and fix there. To leave, yes, regain my independence and dignity, to set out on the City Ring Road, my possessions clasped to my chest, the infinite stars towering above me and the songs of nightingales ringing in my ears. Sally Klee receding ever farther behind me, she caring nothing for me, no, nor I for her, to lope carefree towards the orange dawn and on into the next day and again into the following night, crossing rivers and penetrating woods, to search for and find a new love, a new post, a new function, a new life. A new life. The very words are deadweight on my lips, for what new life could be more exalted than the old, what new function rival that of Sally Klee's ex-lover? No future can equal my past. I turn towards the stairs and almost immediately begin to wonder if I could not convince myself of alternative descriptions of the situation. This afternoon, blighted by my own inadequacy, I acted for the best, it was in both our interests. Sally Klee returning home from a troubled day must have entered her room to discover it bereft of a certain few familiar articles and she must have felt then that her only source of comfort had left her side without a word. Without one word! My hands and feet are on the fourth stair. Surely it is she, not I, who is hurt. And what are explanations but silent, invisible things in your head? I have appropriated more than my fair share of damage and she is silent because she is sulking. It is she who longs for explanations and reassurance. She who longs to be esteemed, stroked, breathed on. Of course! How could I have failed to understand that during our silent meal. She needs *me*. I gain this realisation like a mountaineer a virgin summit and arrive at Sally Klee's open door a little out of breath, less from exertion than from triumph.

Wreathed by the light from her writing lamp she sits with her back to me, elbows resting on the desk, head supported under the chin by her cupped hands. The sheet of paper in her typewriter is crowded with words. It has yet to be pulled clear and laid in the blue clasp file. Standing here directly behind Sally Klee I am struck by a

vivid memory from my earliest infancy. I am staring at
my mother who squats with her back to me and then, for
the first time in my life, I see past her shoulder as through
a mist pale, spectral figures beyond the plate glass, pointing and mouthing silently. I advance noiselessly into the
room and squat down a few feet behind Sally Klee's
chair. Now I am here, it seems an impossible idea she
will ever turn in her chair and notice me.

Two Fragments: March 199-

Saturday

Towards dawn Henry woke, but did not open his eyes. He saw a luminous white mass fold in upon itself, the residue of a dream he could not recall. Superimposed black shapes with arms and legs drifted upwards and away like crows against a blank sky. When he opened his eyes the room was sunk in deep blue light and he was staring into the eyes of his daughter. She stood close to the bed, her head level with his. Pigeons grunted and stirred on the window-ledge. Father and daughter, they stared and neither spoke. Footsteps receded on the street outside. Henry's eyes narrowed. Marie's grew larger, she moved her lips faintly, her tiny body shivered under the white nightgown. She watched her father drift into sleep.

Presently she said, 'I've got a vagina.'

Henry moved his legs and woke again. 'Yes,' he said.

'So I'm a girl, aren't I?'

Henry supported himself on his elbow. 'Go back to bed now, Marie. You're cold.'

She moved away from the bed, out of his reach, and stood facing the window, facing the grey light. 'Are pigeons boys or girls?'

Henry lay on his back and said, 'Boys *and* girls.'

Marie moved closer to the sound of the pigeons and listened. 'Do girl pigeons have a vagina?'

'Yes.'

'Where do they?'

'Where do you think?'

She considered, she listened. She looked back at him over her shoulder. 'Under their feathers?'

'Yes.' She laughed delightedly. The grey light was brightening.

'Into bed now,' Henry said with faked urgency.

She walked towards him. 'In *your* bed, Henry,' she demanded. He moved over for her and pulled back the covers. She climbed in and he watched her fall asleep.

An hour later Henry slipped from the bed without waking the child. He stood beneath the dribbling shower and afterwards paused for a moment in front of a large mirror and regarded his naked dripping body. Lit from one side only by the watery light of first day he appeared to himself sculpted, monumental, capable of superhuman feats.

He dressed hurriedly. When he was pouring coffee in the kitchen he heard loud voices and footsteps on the stairs outside his flat. Automatically he glanced out the window. A light rain was falling and the light was dropping. Henry went to the bedroom to watch out the window. Behind him Marie still slept. The sky was thick and angry.

As far as he could see in either direction the street was filling with people preparing to collect rain-water. They were unrolling canvas tarpaulins, working in twos, in families. It grew darker. They stretched the canvases across the road and secured the ends to drain-pipes and railings. They rolled barrels into the centre of the street to collect water from the tarpaulins. For all this activity there was silence, jealous, competitive silence. As usual fights were breaking out. Space was limited. Beneath Henry's window two figures wrestled. It was hard to make them out at first. Now he saw that one was a heavily built woman, the other a man of slight build in his early twenties. With their arms locked about each other's neck they edged sideways like a monstrous crab. The rain fell in a continuous sheet and the wrestlers were ignored. Their tarpaulins lay in piles at their feet, the disputed space was taken by others. Now they fought for pride alone and a few children gathered round to watch. They rolled to the ground. The woman was suddenly on top, pinning the man to the ground with her knee pressed against his throat. His legs kicked uselessly. A small dog, its pink member erect and vivid in the gloom, threw itself into the struggle. It clasped the man's head between its front paws. Its haunches quivered like plucked strings and its pink tongue flashed from the root. The children laughed and pulled it away.

Marie was out of bed when he turned away from the window. 'What are you doing, Henry?'

'Watching the rain,' he said, and gathered her up in his arms and carried her to the bathroom.

It took an hour to walk to work. They stopped once, half-way across Chelsea bridge. Marie climbed from her push-chair and Henry held her up so she could look down at the river. It was a daily ritual. She gazed in silence and struggled a little when she'd had enough. Thousands walked in the same direction each morning. Henry rarely recognised a friend but if he did they walked together in silence.

The Ministry rose from a vast plain of pavement. The pushchair bumped over green wedges of weed. The stones were cracking and subsiding. Human refuse littered the plain. Vegetables, rotten and trodden down, cardboard boxes flattened into beds, the remains of fires and the carcasses of roasted dogs and cats, rusted tin, vomit, worn tyres, animal excrement. An old dream of horizontal lines converging on the thrusting steel and glass perpendicular was now beyond recall.

The air above the fountain was grey with flies. Men and boys came there daily to squat on the wide concrete rim and defecate. In the distance, along one edge of the plain, several hundred men and women still slept. They were wrapped in striped, brightly coloured blankets which in day time marked out shop space. From that group came the sound of a child crying, carried on the wind. No one stirred. 'Why is that baby crying?' Marie shouted suddenly, and her own voice was lost in that big, miserable place. They hurried on, they were late. They were tiny, the only moving figures on the great expanse.

To save time Henry ran down the stairs to the basement with Marie in his arms. Even before he was through the swing doors someone was saying to him, 'We like them to be on time.' He turned and set Marie down. The play-group leader rested her hand on Marie's head. She was over six feet tall and emaciated, her eyes were sunk deep and broken blood vessels danced on her cheeks. When she spoke again she stretched her lips tightly round her teeth and rose on her toes. 'And if you don't mind ... the subscriptions. Would you care to settle now?' Henry was three months behind. He promised to bring money the next day. She shrugged and took Marie's hand. He watched them pass through a door and caught a glimpse of two black children in a violent embrace. The noise was shrill and deafening, and cut off dead when the door closed behind them.

When, thirty minutes later, Henry began to type the second letter of the morning, he could no longer remember the contents of the first. He worked from the long-hand scrawl of some higher official. When he came to the end of the fifteenth letter, shortly before lunch, he could not remember its beginning. And he did not care to move his eyes up the page to see. He carried the letters into a smaller office and gave them to someone without seeing who it was who took them. Henry returned to his desk, with only minutes now to waste before lunch. All the typists were smoking as they worked and the air was thick and sharp with smoke, not of this day alone but of ten thousand previous days and ten thousand days to come. There seemed no way forward. Henry lit a cigarette and waited.

He descended the sixteen floors to the basement and joined a long queue of parents, mostly mothers, who came in their lunch hour to see their children. It was a murmuring queue of supplicants. They came out of need not duty. They spoke to each other in soft voices about their children while the line shuffled towards the swing doors. Each child had to be signed for. The playgroup leader stood by the doors, by her presence alone conveying a need for silence and order. The parents complied, and signed. Marie was waiting for him just beyond the doors, and when she saw him she raised two clenched fists above her head and made an innocent little dance. Henry signed and took her hand.

The sky had cleared and a sickly warmth rose from the flagstones. The vast plain teemed now like a colony of ants. Above it hung a pale sickle moon, clear against the blue sky. Marie climbed in the pushchair and Henry wheeled her through the crowds.

All those with something to sell crammed on to the plain and spread their goods on coloured blankets. An old woman was selling half-used cakes of soap arranged across a bright yellow rug like precious stones. Marie chose a green piece the size and shape of a chicken's egg. Henry bargained with the woman and brought her down to half her first price. As they exchanged money for soap she made a show of scowls and Marie recoiled from her in surprise. The old woman smiled, reached into her bag and brought out a small present. But Marie climbed back into her pushchair and would not take it. 'Go away,' Marie shouted at the old woman, 'Go away.' They walked on. Henry headed for a far corner of the plain where there was space to sit and eat lunch. He made a wide detour round the fountain, on the rim of which men perched like featherless birds.

They sat on a parapet which ran along one side of the plain and ate bread and cheese. Below them stretched the deserted buildings of Whitehall. Henry asked Marie questions about the playgroup. There were rumours of indoctrination but his questions were casual and un-pressing. 'What did you play with today?'

She told him excitedly of a game with water and a boy who had cried, a boy who always cried. He took from his pocket a small treat, cold, bright yellow, mysteriously curved and laid it in her hands. 'What is it, Henry?'

'It's a banana. You can eat it.' He showed her how to peel the skin away, and told her how they grew in bunches in a far-off country. Later he asked, 'Did the lady read you a story, Marie?'

She turned and stared over the parapet. 'Yes,' she said after a while.

'What was it about?'

She giggled. 'It was about bananas … bananas … bananas.' They began the half-mile walk back to the Ministry and Marie chanted her new word quietly to herself.

Far ahead the crowd was collecting round a point of interest. Some people were running past them to join it and were forming a circle around a compulsive beat, around a man with a drum. By the time Henry and Marie arrived the circle was ten deep and the cries of the man were

muffled. Henry lifted Marie on to his shoulders and pushed
deeper into the crowd. By his clothes the people recognised
him as a Ministry worker and indifferently stood aside. Now
it was possible to see. In the centre of the ring was a squat,
black oil drum. Animal skin was stretched over one end
and the man beside it, a man the size of a great lumbering
bear, banged it with his bare fist. Sacking doused in red
paint wound round his body like a toga. His hair was red
and coarse and reached almost to his waist. The hair on
his bare arms was thick and matted like animal fur. Even
his eyes were red.

He was not shouting words. With each pulse of the drum
he gave out a deep loud growl. He was watching something closely in the crowd and Henry, following his eyeline,
saw a large rusty tin passing from hand to hand and heard
the clink of coins. Then he saw in the crowd a dull flash
of reflected sunlight. It was a long sword, slightly curved
with an ornamental handle. The crowd reached out to
hold it, touch it, assure themselves of its substantiality. It
moved in counter-motion to the biscuit tin. Marie tugged
at Henry's ear and demanded explanations. He pushed
deeper towards the circle till they were second from the
front. The tin came close. Henry felt the man's fierce red
eyes on him and threw in three small coins. The man beat
the drum and roared and the tin passed on.

Marie shivered on Henry's shoulders and he stroked her
bare knees for comfort. Suddenly the man broke into
words, a crude chant on two notes. His words were ponderous and slurred. Henry made them out, and at the
same time saw the girl for the first time. 'Without blood ...
without blood ... without blood ... ' She was standing far
to one side, a girl of about sixteen, naked from the waist
up and barefoot. She stood perfectly still, hands at her
side, feet together, staring at the ground a few feet in front
of her. Her hair too was red, but fine and cropped short.

Round her waist she wore a piece of sacking. She was so pale it was quite possible to believe that she was without blood.

Now the drum took on a steady arterial pulse and the sword was returned to the man. He held it high above his head and glowered at the crowd. Someone from the crowd brought him the biscuit tin. He peered inside and shook his great head. The tin was returned to the crowd and the drum beat accelerated. 'Without blood,' the man shouted. 'Through her belly, out her back, without blood.' The tin appeared in his hands again, and again he refused it. The crowd was desperate. Those at the back pushed forward to throw in money, those who had given shouted at those who had not. Quarrels broke out, but the tin was filling. When it returned the third time it was accepted and the crowd sighed with relief. The drum beat ceased.

By a movement of his head the man ordered the girl, surely his daughter, into the centre of the circle. She stood with the oil drum between her and her father. Henry saw her legs shaking. The crowd was silent, anxious to miss nothing. The cries of vendors reached them across the plain as though from another world. Marie shouted out suddenly, her voice thin with fear, 'What's she going to do?' Henry shushed her, the man was putting the sword into his daughter's hands. He did not take his eyes off her and she seemed powerless to look anywhere but into his face. He hissed something in her ear and she raised the point of the sword to her belly. Her father bent down and emptied the biscuit tin into a leather bag which he slung across his shoulder. The sword shook in the girl's hands and the crowd stirred impatiently.

Henry felt sudden warmth spread across his neck and down his back. Marie had urinated. He lifted her to the ground and at that moment, urged on by her father, the girl pushed the tip of the sword half an inch into her belly. Marie screamed with rage. She beat her fists against Henry's legs. 'Lift me up,' she sobbed. A small coin of crimson, brilliant in the sunlight, spread outwards round the shaft of the sword. Someone in the crowd sneered, 'Without blood.' The father secured the leather bag beneath his toga. He made towards the sword as if to plunge it through his daughter. She collapsed at his feet and the sword clattered on to the pavement. The gigantic man picked it up and shook it at the angry crowd. 'Pigs,' he shouted. 'Greedy pigs.' The crowd was enraged and shouted back. 'Cheat ... murderer ... he's got our money ... '

But they were afraid, for when he pulled his daughter to her feet and dragged her off they scattered to make a path for him. He swung the sword about his head. 'Pigs,' he kept on shouting. 'Get back, you pigs.' A stone was thrown hard and caught him high on the shoulder. He spun round, dropped his daughter and went for the crowd like a madman, sweeping the sword in huge vicious arcs. Henry picked up Marie and ran with the rest of them. When he turned back to look the man was far away, urging his daughter along. The crowd had left him alone with his money. Henry and Marie walked back and found the pushchair on its side. One of the handles was bent.

That evening, on the long walk home, Marie sat quietly and asked no questions. Henry felt anxious for her, but he was too tired to be of use. After the first mile she was asleep. He crossed the river by Vauxhall bridge and stopped halfway across, this time for himself. The Thames was lower than he had ever seen it. Some said that one day the river would dry up and giant bridges would uselessly span fresh meadows. He remained on the bridge ten minutes smoking a cigarette. It was difficult to know what to believe. Many people said that tap water was slow poison.

At home he lit all the candles in the house to dispel Marie's fears. She followed him about closely. He cooked a fish on the paraffin stove and they ate in the bedroom. He talked to Marie about the sea which she had never seen and later he read her a story till she fell asleep on his lap. She woke as he was carrying her to her bed and said, 'What did that lady do with her sword?'

Henry said, 'She danced. She danced with it in her hands.' Marie's clear blue eyes looked deep into his own. He sensed her disbelief and regretted his lie.

He worked late into the night. Towards two o'clock he went to the window in his bedroom and opened it. The moon had sunk and clouds had moved in and covered the stars. He heard a pack of dogs down by the river. To the north he could see the fires burning on the Ministry plain. He wondered if things would change much in his lifetime. Behind him Marie called out in her sleep and laughed.

Sunday

I left Marie with a neighbour and walked northwards across London – a distance of six miles – to a reunion with an old lover. We knew each other from the old times, and it was in their memory rather than for passion that we continued to meet occasionally. On this day our love-making was long and poignantly unsuccessful. After, in a room of dusty sunshine and torn plastic furniture, we spoke of the old times. In a low voice Diane complained of emptiness and foreboding. She wondered which government and which set of illusions were to blame and how it could have been otherwise. Politically Diane was more sophisticated than I was. 'We'll see what happens,' I said. 'But now roll on to your belly.' She told me about her new job, helping an old man with his fish. He was a friend of her uncle's. Each day at dawn she was down at the river to meet his rowing-boat. They loaded a handcart with fish and eels and pushed it to a small street market where the old man had a stall. He went home to sleep and prepare for the night's work, she sold his fish. In the early evening she took the money to his house and perhaps because she was pretty, he insisted they divide the takings evenly. While she spoke I massaged her neck and back. 'Now everything smells of fish,' she cried. I had taken it for the lingering genital smell of another lover – she had many – but I did not say. Her fears and complaints were no different from mine, and yet – or rather, consequently – I said only bland, comfortless things. I worked my thumbs into the thick folds of skin in the small of her back. She sighed. I said, 'It's a job at least.'

I rose from the bed. In the bathroom I gazed into an ancient-looking mirror. My bag of skin lay against the cool rim of the sink. Orgasm, however desultory, brought on the illusion of clarity. The unvarying buzz of an insect sustained my inaction. Making a guess at my silence Diane called out, 'How's your little girl?'

'All right, coming on,' I said. However, I was thinking of my birthday, thirty in ten days' time, and that in turn brought to mind my mother. I stooped to wash. Two years ago there had reached me, through a friend, a letter written on a coarse sheet of pink paper folded tightly and sealed inside a used envelope. My mother named a village in Kent. She was working in the fields, she had milk, cheese, butter and a little meat from the farm. She sent wistful love to her son and grandchild. Since then, in moments of clarity or restlessness – I could not tell – I had made and retracted plans to leave the city with Marie. I calculated the village to be a week's walk away. But each time I made excuses, I forgot my plans. I forgot even the recurrence of my plans and each occasion was freshly determined. Fresh milk, eggs, cheese ... occasional meat. And yet more than the destination, it was the journey itself which excited me. With an odd sense of making my first preparations I washed my feet in the sink.

I returned to the bedroom transformed – as was usual when I made these plans – and was faintly impatient to find it unchanged. Diane's clothes and mine littered the furniture, dust and sunshine and objects packed the room. Diane had not moved since I left the room. She lay on her back on the bed, legs apart, right knee a little crooked, hand resting on her belly, mouth slack with a buried complaint. We failed to please each other, but we did talk. We were sentimentalists. She smiled and said, 'What was that you were singing?' When I told her of my plans she said, 'But I thought you were going to wait until Marie was older.' I remembered that now as merely an excuse for delay. 'She *is* older,' I insisted.

By Diane's bed there stood a low table with a thick glass top within which there was trapped a still cloud of delicate black smoke. On the table there was a telephone, its wire severed at four inches, and beyond that, propped against the wall, a cathode ray tube. The wooden casing, the glass screen and control buttons had long ago been ripped away and now bunches of bright wire curled about the dull metal. There were innumerable breakable objects — vases, ashtrays, glass bowls, Victorian or what Diane called Art Deco. I was never certain of the difference. We all scavenge for serviceable items, but like many others in her minimally privileged part of the city, Diane amassed items without function. She believed in interior decor, in style. We argued about these objects, once even bitterly. 'We no longer craft things,' she had said. 'Nor do we manufacture or mass-produce them. We make nothing, and I like things that are made, by craftsmen or by processes' (she had indicated the telephone), 'it doesn't matter, because they're still the products of human inventiveness and design. And not caring for objects is one step away from not caring for people.'

I had said, 'Collecting these things and setting them out like this amounts to self-love. Without a telephone system telephones are worthless junk.' Diane was eight years older than I. She had insisted that you cannot love other people or accept their love for you unless you love yourself. I thought that was trite, and the discussion ended in silence.

It was growing colder. We got between the sheets, me with my plans and clean feet, she with her fish. 'The point is,' I said referring to Marie's age, 'that you cannot survive now without a plan.' I lay with my head on Diane's arm and she drew me towards her breast. 'I know someone,' she began, and I knew she was introducing a lover, 'who wants to start a radio station. He doesn't know how to generate electricity. He doesn't know anyone who could build a transmitter or repair an old one. And even if he did, he knows there are no radios to pick up his signal. He talks vaguely about repairing old ones, of finding a book that will tell him how to do it. I say to him, "Radio stations cannot exist without an industrial society." And he says, "We'll see about that." You see, it's the programmes he's interested in. He gets other people interested and they sit around talking about programmes. He wants only *live* music. He wants eighteenth-century chamber music in the early morning, but he knows there are no orchestras. In the evenings he meets his Marxist friends and they plan talks, courses, they discuss which line to take. There's a historian who has written a book and wants to read it aloud in twenty-six half-hour instalments.'

'It's no good trying to have the past all over again,' I said after a while. 'I don't care about the past, I want to make a future for Marie and myself.' I stopped and we both laughed, for as I denied the past I lay on Diane's breasts and spoke of living with my mother. It was an old joke between us. We drifted into reminiscences. Surrounded by Diane's mementoes it was easy enough to imagine the world outside the room as it once was, ordered and calamitous. We talked about one of the first days we spent together. I was eighteen, Diane twenty-six. We walked from Camden Town across Regent's Park, along an avenue of bare plane-trees. It was February, cold and bright. We bought tickets to the zoo because we had heard that it was soon to shut down. It was a disappointment, we wandered despondently from one cage, one moated folly of an environment to the next. The cold muted the animals' smell, the brightness illuminated their futility. We regretted the money spent on tickets. After all, the animals simply looked like their names, tigers, lions, penguins, elephants, no more, no less. We passed a better hour in the warm talking and drinking tea, the only customers in a vast café of infinite municipal sadness.

On our way out of the zoo we were drawn by the shouts of schoolchildren towards the chimpanzees. It was a cage in the style of an enormous aviary, a mean parody of the animals forgotten past. Between rhododendron bushes a jungle track curved, an irregular system of bars for swinging spanned the cage and there were two stunted trees. The shouts were for a powerful, bad-tempered male, the cage patriarch, who was terrorising the other chimpanzees. They scattered before him, and were disappearing through a small hole in the wall. Now all that remained was what looked like an elderly mother, perhaps she was a grandmother, round whose belly clung a baby chimpanzee. The male was after her. Screaming, she ran along the track and swung on to the bars. They flew round the cage. He was inches behind her. As her trailing hand left one bar, so his forward hand reached it.

The delighted children danced and screamed as she climbed higher and went faster. The baby clung, its small pink face, half-buried in tit and fur, described wide trajectories in the air. Now the two raced across the ceiling of the cage, the female jabbering as she flew and spattering the bars below with her bright green excrement. Suddenly the male lost interest and permitted his victims to escape through the hole in the wall. The schoolchildren moaned in disappointment. The cage was silent and still, chimpanzees appeared comically at the hole and looked out. The patriarch sat high in one corner gazing with bright, abstracted eyes over his shoulder. Slowly the cage filled and the mother returned with her baby. Glancing warily at her pursuer, she gathered up as much of her excrement as she could find and withdrew to a treetop where she could eat in comfort. From the end of her finger she fed small amounts to the baby. She looked down at the human spectators and stuck out her bright green tongue. The infant huddled against its protectress, the schoolchildren dispersed.

We lay in silence for many minutes after our reminiscences. The bed was small but comfortable and I felt drowsy. My eyes were already closed when Diane said, 'Memories like that don't bother me any more. Everything has changed so much I can hardly believe it was us who were there.' I heard her clearly but I could do no more than grunt in assent. I believed myself to be saying goodbye to Diane. Outside the day was sunny and warm. I leaned out of my car and waved to her where she stood at the window. I found I knew the controls perfectly, of course, I had always known. The car moved forward silently. I felt hungry and drove past restaurants and cafés but I did not stop. I had a destination, a friend in some distant suburb, but I did not know who. What I was driving along was called the Circle Road. The afternoon was warm, the traffic around me swift and agile, the landscape dehumanised and utterly comprehensible. Place names were illuminated on clinical road signs. A glaring tunnel tiled like a urinal swung from left to right through parabolic curves and pitched violently upwards into daylight. Men and women gunned their engines at traffic lights, faulty machines or incompetent drivers would not be tolerated. Through an open window ringed fingers drummed against the side of a car. Before a towering bra advertisement a man scrutinised his watch. Behind him the colossus tugged at her straps with frozen insouciance. The lights changed and we all leapt forward, content and contempt pressed into the set of our lips. I saw a sad boy astride a supermarket horse while his father stood by and smiled.

It was bitterly cold and growing dark. Diane was on the other side of the room lighting a candle. I lay in her bed watching her search for warmer clothes to put on. I felt sorry for her, living alone with all her antiques. We had such easy intimacy but my visits were rare, it was a long walk from south to north and back again, and a little dangerous.

I did not mention my dream. Diane pined for the age of machines and manufacture, for automobiles were once part of the texture of her life. She often spoke of the pleasure of driving a car, of travelling within a set of rules. Stop ... Go ... Fog Ahead. I was an indifferent passenger as a child and in my teens I watched their dwindling numbers from the pavement. Diane longed for rules. I said, 'I suppose I'd better go,' and began to get dressed. We stood shivering by the door.

'Promise me something,' said Diane.

'What is that?'

'That you won't leave for the country without coming to say goodbye.' I promised. We kissed and Diane said, 'I couldn't bear you both to leave without me knowing.'

As usual in the early evening there were a lot of people about. It was cold enough for street-corner fires to be lit and people stood around them and talked. Behind them their children played in the darkness. To make quicker progress I walked in the middle of the street, down long avenues of rusted, broken cars. It was downhill all the way into central London. I crossed the canal and entered Camden Town. I walked to Euston and turned up the Tottenham Court Road. Everywhere it was the same, people came out of their cold houses and huddled round fires. Some groups I passed stood in silence, staring into the flames; it was too early yet to go to sleep. I turned right at Cambridge Circus into Soho. At the corner of Frith Street and Old Compton Street there was a fire and

I stopped to rest and get warm. Two middle-aged men on either side of the fire were arguing passionately through the flames while the rest listened or stood dreaming on their feet. League football was a fading memory. Men like these would beat their brains out, or each other's, attempting to recall details that once came easily to mind. 'I was there, mate. They scored before half-time.' Without moving his feet the other pretended to walk away in disgust. 'Don't talk like daft,' he said. 'It was a goal-less draw.' They began to talk at the same time and it became difficult to listen.

Someone behind and to my right made a movement towards me and I turned. A small Chinaman stood just within the circle of light. His head was onion-shaped, he was smiling and beckoning with large sweeps of his arm, as though I stood on a distant hill-top. I took a couple of paces towards him and said. 'What do you want?' He wore the upper part of an old grey suit, and bright new drainpipe jeans. Where did he get new jeans? 'What do you want?' I said again. The little man breathed and sang at me. 'Come! You come!' Then he stepped out of the ring of light and disappeared.

The Chinaman walked several feet ahead and was barely visible. We crossed Shaftesbury Avenue into Gerrard Street and here I slowed to a shuffle and stretched my hands in front of my face. A few upper-storey windows gleamed dully, they gave a sense of the direction of the street but they shone no light into it. For several minutes I edged forwards, then the Chinaman lit a lamp. He was fifty yards ahead and stood holding the lamp level with his head, waiting. When I reached him he showed me a low doorway blocked by something square and black. It was a cupboard and as the man squeezed past it I saw by his lamp that beyond it there was a steep flight of stairs. The Chinaman hung the lamp inside the doorway. He lifted his end of the cupboard. I lifted mine. It was unnaturally heavy and we had to take it up one step at a time. To co-ordinate our efforts the Chinaman exhorted 'You come' in his breathing, singing voice. We developed a rhythm and left the lamp far below. A long time passed and the stairs seemed to be without end. 'You come ... you come,' the Chinaman sang to me from inside his cupboard. At last a door opened ahead and yellow light and kitchen smells trickled down the stairwell. A taut, tenor voice of indeterminate sex spoke Chinese and somewhere further beyond a child cried.

I sat at a table scattered with biscuit crumbs and salt grains. At the other end of this crowded room the Chinaman was arguing with his wife, a tiny, strained woman with a face of tendons and twisting muscles. Behind them was a boarded-up window and beyond the door was a pile of mattresses and blankets. A few feet from where I sat two male infants, naked but for yellowish vests, stood bow-legged and drooling, watching me, their elbows extended for balance. A girl of about twelve years watched over them. Her face was a creamier version of her mother's, and her dress was her mother's too, far too large and gathered about the waist with a thin plastic belt. From a pot which simmered on a small wood fire came a thin, salty smell, mingling with the milk and urine smell of small children. I was uneasy, I regretted the lost privacy of my walk home in the dark, the contemplation of my plans, but an obscure sense of politeness prevented me from leaving.

I was developing my own version of the argument between man and wife. I knew of Chinese decorum. He was wanting to reward the guest for his help, it was a matter of honour. 'That's nonsense,' she was insisting. 'Look at that thick coat he's wearing. He has more than we do. It would be foolish and sentimental, when we have so little, to make gifts to such a man, however kind.'

'But he helped us,' her husband seemed to counter. 'We can't send him away with nothing. At least let's give him some supper.'

'No, no. There isn't enough.' The discussion was formal and restrained, barely rising above a whisper. Dissent was expressed by monologues which overlapped, the undulating tendons in the woman's neck, the man's left hand which clenched and unclenched. Silently I urged the woman on. I wished to be dismissed with gentle, courteous handshakes, never to return. I would walk southwards home and climb into bed. One of the infants, eyes fixed on mine, began to stagger towards me. I looked to the girl to intercept, who complied, but sullenly, and I suspected she held back longer than was necessary.

The argument was over, the woman was bending over a pile of mattresses preparing a bed for the babies, and her husband was watching her from a chair next to mine. The girl leaned against the wall and made a melancholy examination of her fingers. I played with the crumbs and grains. The Chinaman turned and smiled faintly at me. Then he addressed to his daughter an unbroken sentence of apparent complexity, the final section of which rose steadily in pitch while the expression on his face remained fixed. The girl looked at me and said dully, 'Dad says you gotta eat wiv us.' To clarify this her father pointed at my mouth and then to the pot. 'You come,' he said with enthusiasm. In the corner the mother spoke sharply to her children who lay at either end of a small mattress crying sleepily. I looked steadily in her direction hoping to catch her eye and have her approbation. Bored, the girl resumed her position against the wall, her father sat with folded arms and filmy, vacant eyes. I said, 'What does your mother think?' The girl shrugged and did not look up from her fingernails. Against hers my voice sounded hollow and cultivated, suggestive of laconic manipulation. 'What were your parents talking about just now?' She looked at the black cupboard. 'Mum says Dad paid too much for it.'

I decided to leave. To the Chinaman I pantomimed by making a sick face and pointing to my stomach that I was not hungry. My host seemed to take this to mean that I was too hungry to wait till suppertime. He spoke rapidly to his daughter, and when she answered he cut her off angrily. She shrugged and crossed to the fire. The room filled with a thin, hot, animal smell which resembled the taste of blood. I twisted round in my chair to speak to the girl. 'I don't want to offend your parents, but tell your Dad I'm not hungry and I've got to go.'

'I told him that already,' she said, and ladled something into a large white bowl which she set before me. She seemed to relish my situation. 'Neither of 'em listen,' she said, and returned to her part of the wall.

In a large quantity of clear hot water several dun-coloured globes, partially submerged, drifted and collided noiselessly. The Chinaman's face puckered in encouragement. 'You come.' I was aware of the woman watching me from her side of the room. 'What is it?' I asked the girl.

'It's muck,' she said vaguely. Then she changed her mind and hissed vehemently. 'It's *piss*.' With a low chuckle and small flourish of his dry hands the Chinaman appeared to celebrate his daughter's mastery of a difficult language. Watched by all the family I picked up the spoon. The babies were quiet in their corner. I took two rapid sips and smiled up at the parents through the unswallowed liquid. 'Good,' I said at last, and then to the girl. 'Tell them it's good.' Once again not looking up from her fingernails she said, 'I'd leave it if I was you.' I manoeuvred one of the globes on to my spoon, it was surprisingly heavy. I did not ask the girl what it was, for I knew what she would say.

I swallowed it and stood up. I offered my hand to the Chinaman in farewell, but he and his wife stared and did not move. 'G'wan, just go,' the girl said with resignation. I moved slowly round the table, fearful of vomiting. As I reached the door something the girl said caused the mother to become suddenly angry. She was shouting at her husband and pointing at my bowl from which there still rose, as if in accusation, a fine white trace of steam. The Chinaman sat quietly, apparently indifferent. Now the furious woman lay into her daughter, who abruptly turned her back and would not listen. Father and daughter seemed to wait for silence for a cord to snap in the tiny woman's neck, and I too waited, half-concealed by the cupboard, hoping to go forward and ease the situation and my conscience with friendly goodbyes. But the room and its people were an unmoving tableau. Only the shouting carried forward so I slipped away unnoticed down the stairs.

The lamp still burned above the doorway. Knowing the difficulty of finding paraffin I turned it out, then stepped into the black street.

Dead As They Come

❧❧❧

I do not care for posturing women. But she *struck* me. I had to stop and look at her. The legs were well apart, the right foot boldly advanced, the left trailing with studied casualness. She held her right hand before her, almost touching the window, the fingers thrusting up like a beautiful flower. The left hand she held a little behind her and seemed to push down playful lapdogs. Head well back, a faint smile, eyes half-closed with boredom or pleasure. I could not tell. Very artificial the whole thing, but then I am not a simple man. She was a beautiful woman. I saw her most days, sometimes two or three times. And of course she struck other postures as the mood took her. Sometimes as I hurried by (I am a man in a hurry) I allowed myself a quick glance and she seemed to beckon me, to welcome me out of the cold. Other days I remember seeing her in that tired, dejected passivity which fools mistake for femininity.

I began to take notice of the clothes she wore. She was a fashionable woman, naturally. In a sense it was her job. But she had none of the sexless, mincing stiffness of those barely animated clothes-hangers who display *haute couture* in stuffy salons to the sound of execrable musak. No, she was another class of being. She did not exist merely to present a style, a current mode. She was above that, she was *beyond* that. Her clothes were peripheral to her beauty. She would have looked good dressed in old paper bags.

She disdained her clothes, she discarded them every day for others. Her beauty shone through those clothes . . . and yet they were beautiful clothes. It was autumn. She wore capes of deep russet browns, or twirling peasant skirts of orange and green, or harsh trouser suits of burnt ochre. It was spring. She wore skirts of passion-fruit gingham, white calico shirts or lavish dresses of cerulean green and blue. Yes, I noticed her clothes, for she understood, as only the great portrait painters of the eighteenth century understood, the sumptuous possibilities of fabric, the subtleties of folds, the nuance of crease and hem. Her body in its rippling changes of posture, adapted itself to the unique demands of each creation; with breathless grace the lines of her perfect body played tender counterpoint with the shifting arabesques of sartorial artifice.

But I digress. I bore you with lyricism. The days came and passed. I saw her this day and not that, and perhaps twice on another day. Imperceptibly seeing her and not seeing her became a factor in my life, and then before I knew it, it passed from factor to structure. Would I see her today? Would all my hours and minutes be redeemed? Would she look at me? Did she remember me from one time to another? Was there a future for us together ... would I ever have the courage to approach her? Courage! What did all my millions mean now, what now of my wisdom matured by the ravages of three marriages? I loved her ... I wished to possess her. And to possess her it seemed I would have to buy her.

I must tell you something about myself. I am wealthy. Possibly there are ten men resident in London with more money than I. Probably there are only five or six. Who cares? I am rich and I made my money on the telephone. I shall be forty-five on Christmas Day. I have been married three times, each marriage lasting, in chronological order, eight, five and two years. These last three years I have not been married and yet I have not been idle. I have not paused. A man of forty-four has no time to pause. I am a man in a hurry. Each throb of jism from the seminal vesicles, or wherever it originates, lessens the total allowance of my lifespan by one. I have no time for the analysis, the self-searching of frenzied relationships, the unspoken accusation, the silent defence. I do not wish to be with women who have an urge to talk when we've finished our coupling. I want to lie still in peace and clarity. Then I want to put my shoes and socks on and comb my hair and go about my business. I prefer silent women who take their pleasure with apparent indifference. All day long there are voices around me, on the telephone, at lunches, at business conferences. I do not want voices in my bed. I am not a simple man, I repeat, and this is not a simple world. But in this respect at least my requisites are simple, perhaps even facile. My predilection is for pleasure unmitigated by the yappings and whinings of the soul.

Or rather it was, for that was all before ... before I loved *her*, before I knew the sickening elation of total self-destruction for a meaningless cause. What do I, now, forty-five on Christmas Day, care for meaning? Most days I passed by her shop and looked in at her. Those early days when a glance was sufficient and I hurried on to meet this business friend or that lover ... I can pick out no time when I knew myself to be in love. I have described how a factor in my life became a structure, it merged as orange to red in the rainbow. Once I was a man hurrying by a shop window and glancing carelessly in. Then I was a man in love with ... simply, I was a man in love. It happened over many months. I began to linger by the window. The others ... the other women in the shop window display meant nothing to me. Wherever my Helen stood I could pick her out at a glance. They were mere dummies (oh my love) beneath contempt. Life was generated in her by the sheer charge of her beauty. The delicate mould of her eyebrow, the perfect line of her nose, the smile, the eyes half-closed with boredom or pleasure (how could I tell?). For a long time I was content to look at her through the glass, happy to be within a few feet of her. In my madness I wrote her letters, yes, I even did that and I still have them. I called her Helen ('Dear Helen, give me a sign. I know you know' etc.). But soon I loved her completely and wished to possess her, own her, absorb her, eat her. I wanted her in my arms and in my bed, I longed that she should open her legs to me. I could not rest till I was between her pale thighs, till my tongue had prised those lips. I knew that soon I would have to enter the shop and ask to buy her.

Simple, I hear you say. You're a rich man. You could buy the shop if you wanted. You could buy the street. Of course I could buy the street, and many other streets too. But listen. This was no mere business transaction. I was not about to acquire a site for redevelopment. In business you make offers, you take risks. But in this matter I could not risk failure, for I wanted my Helen, I *needed* my Helen. My profound fear was that my desperation would give me away. I could not be sure that in negotiating the sale I could keep a steady hand. If I blurted out too high a price the shop manager would want to know why. If it was valuable to me, why then, he would naturally conclude (for was he not a business man too?) it must be valuable to someone else. Helen had been in that shop many months. Perhaps, and this thought began to torment my every waking minute, they would take her away and destroy her.

I knew I must act soon and I was afraid.

I chose Monday, a quiet day in any shop. I was not sure whether quietness was on my side. I could have had Saturday, a busy day, but then, a quiet day ... a busy

day ... my decisions countered each other like parallel
mirrors. I had lost many hours of sleep, I was rude to my
friends, virtually impotent with my lovers, my business
skills were beginning to deteriorate, I had to choose and
I chose Monday. It was October, raining a fine, bitter
drizzle. I dismissed my chauffeur for the day and drove to
the shop. Shall I slavishly follow the foolish conventions
and describe it to you, the first home of my tender Helen?
I do not really care to. It was a large shop, a store, a
department store and it dealt seriously and solely in
clothes and related items for women. It had moving stair-
cases and a muffled air of boredom. Enough. I had a plan.
I walked in.

How many details of this negotiation must be set down
before that moment when I held my precious in my arms?
A few and quickly. I spoke to an assistant. She consulted
with another. They fetched a third, and the third sent a
fourth for a fifth who turned out to be the under-
manageress in charge of window design. They clustered
round me like inquisitive children, sensing my wealth and
power but not my anxiety. I warned them all I had a
strange request and they shifted uneasily from one foot to
the other and avoided my eye. I addressed these five
women urgently. I wanted to buy one of the coats in the
window display, I told them. It was for my wife, I told
them, and I also wanted the boots and scarf that went
with the coat. It was my wife's birthday, I said. I wanted
the dummy (ah my Helen) on which these clothes were
displayed in order to show off the clothes to their best
advantage. I confided in them my little birthday trick.
My wife would open the bedroom door lured there by
some trivial domestic matter invented by myself, and there
would stand ... could they not see it? I recreated the scene
vividly for them. I watched them closely. I brought them
on. They lived through the thrill of a birthday surprise.

They smiled, they glanced at each other. They risked glancing into my eyes. What a kind husband was this! They became, each one, my wife. And of course I was willing to pay a little extra ... but no, the under-manageress would not hear of it. Please accept it with the compliments of the shop. The under-manageress led me towards the window display. She led, and I followed through a blood-red mist. Perspiration dribbled from the palms of my hands. My eloquence had drained away, my tongue glued to my teeth and all I could do was feebly lift my hand in the direction of Helen. 'That one,' I whispered.

Once I was a man hurrying by a shop window and glancing carelessly in ... then I was a man in love, a man carrying his love in his arms through the rain to a waiting car. True, they had offered in the shop to fold and pack the clothes to save them from creasing. But show me the man who will carry his true love naked through the streets in an October rain. How I blabbered with joy as I bore Helen through the streets. And how she hung close to me, clinging tightly to my lapels like a newborn monkey. Oh, my sweetness. Gently I laid her across the back seat of my car and gently drove her home.

At home I had everything prepared. I knew she would want to rest as soon as we came in. I brought her into the bedroom, removed her boots and settled her down between the crisp white bed linen. I kissed her softly on the cheek and before my eyes she fell into a deep slumber. For a couple of hours I busied myself in the library, catching up on important business. I felt serene now, I was illuminated by a steady inner glow. I was capable of intense concentration. I tiptoed into the bedroom where she lay. In sleep her features dissolved into an expression of great tenderness and understanding. Her lips were slightly apart. I knelt down and kissed them. Back in the library

I sat in front of a log fire with a glass of port in my hand. I reflected on my life, my marriages, my recent desperation. All the unhappiness of the past seemed now to have been necessary to make the present possible. I had my Helen now. She lay sleeping in my bed, in my house. She cared for no one else. She was mine.

Ten o'clock came and I slipped into bed beside her. I did it quietly, but I knew she was awake. It is touching now to recall that we did not immediately make love. No, we lay side by side (how warm she was) and we talked. I told her of the time I had first seen her, of how my love for her had grown and of how I had schemed to secure her release from the shop. I told her of my three marriages, my business and my love affairs. I was determined to keep no secrets from her. I told her of the things I had been thinking about as I sat in front of the fire with my glass of port. I spoke of the future, our future together. I told her I loved her, yes I think I told her that many times. She listened with the quiet intensity I was to learn to respect in her. She stroked my hand, she gazed wonderingly into my eyes. I undressed her. Poor girl. She had no clothes on under her coat, she had nothing in the world but me. I drew her close to me, her naked body against mine, and as I did so I saw her wide-eyed look of fear ... she was a virgin. I murmured in her ear. I assured her of my gentleness, my expertise, my control. Between her thighs I caressed with my tongue the fetid warmth of her virgin lust. I took her hand and set her pliant fingers about my throbbing manhood (oh her cool hands). 'Do not be afraid,' I whispered, 'do not be afraid.' I slid into her easily, quietly like a giant ship into night berth. The quick flame of pain I saw in her eyes was snuffed by long agile fingers of pleasure. I have never known such pleasure, such total accord ... almost total, for I must confess there was a shadow I could not dispel. She had been a virgin, now she was a demanding lover. She demanded the orgasm I could not give her, she would not let me go, she would not permit me to rest. On and on through the night, she forever teetering on the edge of that cliff, release in that most gentle death ... but nothing I did, and I did everything, I gave everything, could bring her to it. At last, it must have been five o'clock in the morning, I broke away from her, delirious with fatigue, anguished and hurt by my failure. Once again we lay side by side, and this time I felt in her silence inarticulate rebuke. Had I not brought her from the shop where she had lived in relative peace, had I not brought her to this bed and boasted to her of my expertise? I took her hand. It was stiff and unfriendly. It came to me in a panic-filled moment that Helen might leave me. It was a fear that was to return much later. There was nothing to stop her. She had no money, virtually no skills. No clothes. But she could leave me all the same. There were other men. She could go back and work in the shop. 'Helen,' I said urgently. 'Helen ... ' She lay perfectly still, seeming to hold her breath. 'It will come, you see, it will come,' and with that I was inside her again, moving slowly, imperceptibly, bringing her with me every step of the way. It took an hour of slow acceleration, and as the grey October dawn pierced the brooding London clouds she died, she came, she left this sublunary world ... her first orgasm. Her limbs went rigid, her eyes stared into nowhere and a deep inner spasm swept through her like an ocean wave. Then she slept in my arms.

I woke late the following morning. Helen still lay across my arm but I managed to slip out of bed without waking her. I put on a particularly resplendent dressing-gown, a present from my second wife, and went into the kitchen to make myself coffee. I felt myself to be a different man. I looked at the objects around me, the Utrillo on the kitchen wall, a famous forgery of a Rodin statuette, yesterday's newspapers. They radiated originality, unfamiliarity. I wanted to touch things. I ran my hands over the grain of the kitchen table top. I took delight in pouring my coffee beans into the grinder and in taking from the fridge a ripe grapefruit. I was in love with the world, for I had found my perfect mate. I loved Helen and I knew myself to be loved. I felt free. I read the morning paper at great speed and later in the same day could still remember names of foreign ministers and the countries they represented. I dictated half a dozen letters over the phone, shaved, showered and dressed. When I looked in on Helen she was still asleep, exhausted by pleasure. Even when she woke she would not want to get up till she had some clothes to wear. I had my chauffeur drive me to the West End and I spent the afternoon there buying clothes. It would be crude of me to mention how much I spent, but let me say that few men earn as much in a year. However, I did not buy her a bra. I have always despised them as objects, and yet only student girls and New Guinea natives seem to do without them. Furthermore my Helen did not like them either, which was fortunate.

She was awake when I returned. I had my chauffeur carry the parcels into the dining room and then I dismissed him. I myself carried the parcels from the dining room to the bedroom. Helen was delighted. Her eyes gleamed and she was breathless for joy. Together we chose what she was to wear that evening, a long, pure silk evening dress of pale blue. Leaving her to contemplate what amounted to over two hundred separate items, I hurried into the kitchen to prepare a lavish meal. As soon as I had a spare few minutes I returned to help Helen dress. She stood quite still, quite relaxed while I stood back to admire her. It was of course a perfect fit. But more than that I saw once more her genius for *wearing* clothes, I was beauty in another being as no man has ever seen it, I saw ... it was art, it was the total consummation of line and form that art alone can realise. She seemed luminescent. We stood in silence and gazed into one another's eyes. Then I asked her if she would like me to show her round the house.

I brought her into the kitchen first. I demonstrated its many gadgets. I pointed out the Utrillo on the wall (she was not very fond, I found out later, of painting). I showed her the Rodin forgery and I even offered to let her hold it in her hand but she demurred. Next I took her into the bathroom and showed her the sunken marble bath and how to operate the taps that made the water spew from the mouths of alabaster lions. I wondered if she thought that a little vulgar. She said nothing. I ushered her into the dining room ... once again paintings which I rather bored her with. I showed her my study, my first folio Shakespeares, assorted rarities and many telephones. Then the conference room. There was no need for her to see it really. Perhaps by this time I was beginning to show off a little. Finally the vast living space I simply call the room. Here I spend my leisure hours. I shall not hurl more details at you like so many over-ripe tomatoes ... it is comfortable and not a little exotic.

I sensed immediately that Helen liked the room. She stood in the doorway, hands by her side taking it all in. I brought her over to a large soft chair, sat her down and poured her the drink she so much needed, a dry martini. Then I left her and for the next hour devoted my full attention to the cooking of our meal. What passed that evening was quite certainly the most civilised few hours I have ever shared with a woman or, for that matter, with another person. I have cooked many meals in my home for lady friends. Without hesitation I describe myself as an

excellent cook. One of the very best. But until this particular occasion these evenings have always been dogged by
my guest's conditioned guilt that it was I in the kitchen
and not she, that it was I who carried in the dishes and
carried them away at the end. And throughout my guest
would express continual surprise that I, thrice divorced
and a man to boot, was capable of such triumphs of
cuisine. Not so Helen. She was my guest and that was the
end of it. She did not attempt to invade my kitchen, she
did not perpetually coo, 'Is there something I can *do*?' She
sat back as a guest should and let herself be served by me.
Yes, and the conversation. With those other guests of mine
I always felt conversation to be an obstacle course over
ditches and fences of contradiction, competition, misunderstanding and so on. My ideal conversation is one
which allows both participants to develop their thoughts
to their fullest extent, uninhibitedly, without endlessly
defining and refining premises and defending conclusions.
Without ever reaching conclusions. With Helen I could
converse ideally, I could *talk* to her. She sat quite still, her
eyes fixed at a point several inches in front of her plate,
and listened. I told her many things I had never spoken
out loud before. Of my childhood, my father's death
rattle, my mother's terror of sexuality, my own sexual
initiation with an elder cousin; I spoke of the state of the
world, of the nation, of decadence, liberalism, contem-
porary novels, of marriage, ecstasy and disease. Before we
knew it five hours had passed and we had drunk four
bottles of wine and half a bottle of port. Poor Helen. I had
to carry her to bed and undress her. We lay down, our
limbs entwined and we could do nothing more than fall
into the deepest, most contented sleep.

So ended our first day together, and thus was the
pattern set for many happy months to follow. I was a
happy man. I divided my time between Helen and making

money. The latter I carried through with effortless success. In fact so rich did I become over this period that the government of the day felt it was dangerous for me not to have an influential post. I accepted the knighthood, of course, and Helen and I celebrated in grand style. But I refused to serve the government in any capacity, so thoroughly did I associate it with my second wife, who appeared to wield great influence among its front bench. Autumn turned to winter and then soon there was blossom on the almond trees in my garden, soon the first tender green leaves were appearing on my avenue of oaks. Helen and I lived in perfect harmony which nothing could disturb. I made money, I made love, I talked, Helen listened.

But I was a fool. Nothing lasts. Everyone knows that, but no one believes there are not exemptions. The time has come, I regret, to tell you of my chauffeur, Brian.

Brian was the perfect chauffeur. He did not speak unless spoken to, and then only to concur. He kept his past, his ambitions, his character a secret, and I was glad because I did not wish to know where he came from, where he was going or who he thought he was. He drove competently and outrageously fast. He always knew where to park. He was always at the front of any queue of traffic, and he was rarely in a queue. He knew every short cut, every street in London. He was tireless. He would wait up for me all night at an address, without recourse to cigarettes or pornographic literature. He kept the car, his boots and his uniform spotless. He was pale, thin and neat and I guessed his age to be somewhere between eighteen and thirty-five.

Now it might surprise you to know that, proud as I was of her, I did not introduce Helen to my friends. I introduced her to no one. She did not seem to need any company other than mine and I was content to let matters rest. Why should I begin to drag her round the tedious social circuit of wealthy London? And, furthermore, she was rather shy, even of me at first. Brian was not made an exception of. Without making too obvious a secret of it, I did not let him enter a room if Helen was in there. And if I wanted Helen to travel with me then I dismissed Brian for the day (he lived over the garage) and drove the car myself.

All very clear and simple. But things began to go wrong and I can remember vividly the day it all began. Towards the middle of May I came home from a uniquely tiring and exasperating day. I did not know it then (I suspected it) but I had lost almost half a million pounds due to an error that was completely my own. Helen was sitting in her favourite chair doing nothing in particular, and there was something in her look as I came through the door, something so elusive, so indefinably cool that I had to pretend to ignore it. I drank a couple of scotches and felt better. I sat down beside her and began to tell her of my day, of what had gone wrong, how it had been my fault, how I had impulsively blamed someone else and had to apologise later ... and so on, the caries of a bad day which one has the right to display only to one's mate. But I had been speaking for a little less than thirty-five minutes when I realised that Helen was not listening at all. She was gazing woodenly at her hands which lay across her knees. She was far, far away. It was such a dreadful realisation that I could do nothing for the moment (I was paralysed) but carry on talking. And then I could stand it no more. I stopped mid-sentence and stood up. I walked out the room, slamming the door behind me. At no point did Helen look up from her hands. I was furious, too furious to talk to her. I sat out in the kitchen drinking from the bottle of scotch I had remembered to bring with me. Then I had a shower.

By the time I went back into the room I felt considerably better. I was relaxed, a little drunk and ready to forget the whole matter. Helen too seemed more amenable. At first I was going to ask her what the trouble had been, but we started talking about my day again and in no time we were our old selves again. It seemed pointless going back over things when we were getting on so well. But an hour after dinner the front door bell rang – a rare occurrence in the evening. As I got up from my chair I happened to glance across at Helen and I saw pass across her face that same look of fear she had the night we first made love. It was Brian at the door. He had in his hand a piece of paper for me to sign. Something in connection with the car, something that could have waited till the morning. As I glanced over what it was I was supposed to sign, I saw out of the corner of my eye that Brian was surreptitiously peering over my shoulder into the hallway. 'Looking for something?' I said sharply. 'No sir,' he said. I signed and closed the door. I remembered that because the car was at the garage for servicing Brian had been at home all day. I had taken a taxi to my offices. This fact and Helen's strangeness ... such a sickness came over me when I associated the two that I thought for a moment I was going to vomit and I hurried into the bathroom.

However, I did not vomit. Instead I looked into the mirror. I saw there a man who in less than seven months would be forty-five, a man with three marriages etched about his eyes, the corner of whose mouth drooped downwards from a lifetime talking on the phone. I splashed cold water on my face and joined Helen in the room. 'That was Brian,' I said. She said nothing, she could not look at me. My own voice sounded nasal and toneless. 'He doesn't usually call in the evenings ... ' And still she said nothing. What did I expect? That she suddenly be of a mind to confess an affair with my chauffeur? Helen was a silent woman, she did not find it hard to conceal her feelings.

Nor could I confess what I felt. I was too afraid of being right. I could not bear to hear her confirm the very idea that threatened again to make me vomit. I merely threw out my remarks to make her shore up her pretence ... I so badly wanted to hear it all denied even while knowing the denial to be false. In short, I understood myself to be in Helen's power.

That night we did not sleep together. I made myself up a bed in one of the guest rooms. I did not want to sleep alone, in fact the idea was hateful to me. I suppose (I was so confused) that I wanted to go through the motions so that Helen would ask me what I was doing. I wanted to hear her express surprise that after all these happy months together I was suddenly, without one word being said, making my bed in another room. I wanted to be told not to be foolish, to come to bed, our bed. But she said nothing, absolutely nothing. She took it all for granted ... this was the situation now and no longer could we share a bed. Her silence was deadly confirmation. Or was there a slender possibility (I lay awake in my new bed) that she was simply angry at my moodiness. Now I was really confused. On and on into the night I turned the matter over in my mind. Perhaps she had never even seen Brian. Could the entire matter be of my own imagining? After all, I had had a bad day. But that was absurd, for here was the reality of the situation ... separate beds ... and yet what *should* I have done? What should I have said? I considered every possibility, good lines, cunning silences, terse aphoristic remarks that ripped away at the flimsy veil of appearance. Was she awake now like me, thinking about all this? Or was she fast asleep? How could I find out without appearing to be awake? What would happen **if** she left me? I was completely at her mercy.

I should bankrupt language if I tried to convey the texture of my existence over the following weeks. It had the arbitrary horror of a nightmare, I seemed a roast on a spit which Helen turned slowly with a free hand. It would be wrong of me to attempt to argue in retrospect that the situation was of my own making; but I do know now that I could have ended my misery sooner. It became established that I slept in the guest room. My pride prevented me from returning to our nuptial bed. I wanted Helen to take the initiative on that. It was she after all who had so much explaining to do. I was adamant on this point, it was my only certainty in a time of bleak confusion. I had to hang on tightly to something ... and you see I survived. Helen and I barely talked. We were cold and distant. Each avoided the other's eye. My folly was in thinking that if I remained silent long enough it would somehow break her down and make her want to speak to me, to tell me what she thought was happening to us. And so I roasted. At night I woke from bad dreams shouting and I sulked in the afternoons and tried to think it all out clearly. I had to carry on my business. Often I had to be out of the house, sometimes hundreds of miles away, certain that Brian and Helen were celebrating my absence. Sometimes I phoned home from hotels or airport lounges. No one ever answered, and yet I heard between each throb of the electronic tones Helen in the bedroom gasping with mounting pleasure. I lived in a black valley on the verge of tears. The sight of a small child playing with her dog, the setting sun reflected in a river, a poignant line of advertising copy were enough to dissolve me. When I returned home from business trips, desolate, craving friendship and love, I sensed from the moment I stepped through the door that Brian had been there not long before me. Nothing tangible beyond the *feel* of him in the air, something in the arrangement of the bed, some different smell in the bathroom, the position of the decanter of scotch on its tray. Helen pretended not to see me as I prowled in anguish from room

to room, she pretended not to hear my sobs in the bathroom. It might be asked why I did not dismiss my
chauffeur. The answer is simple. I feared that if Brian left
Helen would follow. I gave my chauffeur no indications of
my feelings. I gave him his orders and he drove me,
maintaining as he always had his faceless obsequiousness.
I observed nothing different in his behaviour, though I
did not care to regard him too closely. It is my belief that
he never knew that I knew, and this at least gave me the
illusion of power over him.

But these are shadowy, peripheral subtleties. Essentially
I was a disintegrating man, I was coming apart. I was
falling asleep at the telephone. My hair began to loose
itself from my scalp. My mouth filled with cankers and
my breath had about it the stench of a decaying carcass.
I observed my business friends take a step backwards
when I spoke. I nurtured a vicious boil in my anus. I was
losing. I was beginning to understand the futility of my
silent waiting games with Helen. In reality there was no
situation between us to play with. All day long she sat in
her chair if I was in the house. Sometimes she sat there all
night. On many occasions I would have to leave the house
early in the morning, leave her sitting in her chair gazing
at the figures in the carpet; and when I returned home
late at night she would be still there. Heaven knows I
wanted to help her. I loved her. But I could do nothing
till she helped me. I was locked in the miserable dungeon
of my mind and the situation seemed utterly hopeless.
Once I was a man hurrying by a shop window and glancing carelessly in, now I was a man with bad breath, boils
and cankers. I was coming apart.

In the third week of this nightmare, when there seemed
nothing else I could do, I broke the silence. It was all or
nothing. Throughout that day I walked in Hyde Park
summoning the remaining shreds of my reason, my will

power, my suaveness for the confrontation I had decided would take place that evening. I drank a little less than a third of a bottle of scotch, and towards seven o'clock I tiptoed to her bedroom where she had been lying for the past two days. I knocked softly, then, hearing no reply, entered. She lay fully dressed on the bed, arms by her side. She wore a pale cotton smock. Her legs were well apart and her head inclined against a pillow. There was barely a gleam of recognition when I stood before her. My heart was pounding wildly and the stench of my breath filled the room like poisonous smoke. 'Helen,' I said, and had to stop to clear my throat. 'Helen, we can't go on like this. It's time we talked.' And then, without giving her a chance to reply, I told her everything. I told her I knew about her affair. I told her about my boil. I knelt at her bedside. 'Helen,' I cried, 'it's meant so much to both of us. We must fight to save it.' There was silence. My eyes were closed and I thought I saw my own soul recede from me across a vast black void till it was a pinprick of red light. I looked up, I looked into her eyes and saw there quiet, naked contempt. It was all over, and I conceived in that frenzied instant two savage and related desires. To rape and destroy her. With one sudden sweep of my hand I ripped the smock clean off her body. She had nothing on underneath. Before she had time to even draw breath I was on her, I was in her, rammed deep inside while my right hand closed about her tender white throat. With my left I smothered her face with the pillow.

I came as she died. That much I can say with pride. I know her death was a moment of intense pleasure to her. I heard her shouts through the pillow. I will not bore you with rhapsodies on my own pleasure. It was a transfiguration. And now she lay dead in my arms. It was some minutes before I comprehended the enormity of my deed. My dear, sweet, tender Helen lay dead in my arms, dead and pitifully naked. I fainted. I awoke what seemed many hours later, I saw the corpse and before I had time to turn my head I vomited over it. Like a sleepwalker I drifted into the kitchen, I made straight for the Utrillo and tore it to shreds. I dropped the Rodin forgery into the garbage disposal. Now I was running like a naked madman from room to room destroying whatever I could lay my hands on. I stopped only to finish the scotch. Vermeer, Blake, Richard Dadd, Paul Nash, Rothke, I tore, trampled, mangled, kicked, spat and urinated on … my precious possessions … oh my precious … I danced, I sang, I laughed … I wept long into the night.

In Between the Sheets

※>>※<<※

That night Stephen Cooke had a wet dream, the first in many years. Afterwards he lay awake on his back, hands behind his head, while its last images receded in the darkness and his cum, strangely located across the small of his back, turned cold. He lay still till the light was blueish-grey, and then he took a bath. He lay there a long time too, staring sleepily at his bright body under water.

That preceding day he had kept an appointment with his wife in a fluorescent café with red formica table tops. It was five o'clock when he arrived and almost dark. As he expected he was there before her. The waitress was an Italian girl, nine or ten years old perhaps, her eyes heavy and dull with adult cares. Laboriously she wrote out the word 'coffee' twice on her notepad, tore the page in half and carefully laid one piece on his table, face downwards. Then she shuffled away to operate the vast and gleaming Gaggia machine. He was the café's only customer.

His wife was observing him from the pavement outside. She disliked cheap cafés and she would make sure he was there before she came in. He noticed her as he turned in his seat to take his coffee from the child. She stood behind the shoulder of his own reflected image, like a ghost, half-hidden in a doorway across the street. No doubt she believed he could not see out of a bright café into the darkness. To reassure her he moved his chair to give her a more complete view of his face. He stirred his coffee and

watched the waitress who leaned against the counter in a
trance, and who now drew a long silver thread from her
nose. The thread snapped and settled on the end of her
forefinger, a colourless pearl. She glared at it briefly and
spread it across her thighs, so finely it disappeared.

When his wife came in she did not look at him at first.
She went straight to the counter and ordered a coffee
from the girl and carried it to the table herself.

'I wish,' she hissed as she unwrapped her sugar, 'you
wouldn't pick places like this.' He smiled indulgently and
downed his coffee in one. She finished hers in careful
pouting sips. Then she took a small mirror and some
tissues from her bag. She blotted her red lips and swabbed
from an incisor a red stain. She crumpled the tissue into her
saucer and snapped her bag shut. Stephen watched the
tissue absorb the coffee slop and turn grey. He said, 'Have
you got another one of those I can have?' She gave him
two.

'You're not going to cry are you?' At one such meeting
he had cried. He smiled. 'I want to blow my nose.' The
Italian girl sat down at a table near theirs and spread out
several sheets of paper. She glanced across at them, and
then leaned forwards till her nose was inches from the
table. She began to fill in columns of numbers. Stephen
murmured, 'She's doing the accounts.'

His wife whispered, 'It shouldn't be allowed, a child of
that age.' Finding themselves in rare agreement, they
looked away from each other's faces.

'How's Miranda?' Stephen said at last.

'She's all right.'

'I'll be over to see her this Sunday.'

'If that's what you want.'

'And the other thing ... ' Stephen kept his eyes on the
girl who dangled her legs now and day-dreamed. Or
perhaps she was listening.

'Yes?'

'The other thing is that when the holidays start I want Miranda to come and spend a few days with me.'

'She doesn't want to.'

'I'd rather hear that from her.'

'She won't tell you herself. You'll make her feel guilty if you ask her.' He banged the table hard with his open hand.

'Listen!' He almost shouted. The child looked up and Stephen felt her reproach. 'Listen,' he said quietly, 'I'll speak to her on Sunday and judge for myself.'

'She won't come,' said his wife, and snapped shut her bag once more as if their daughter lay curled up inside. They both stood up. The girl stood up too and came over to take Stephen's money, accepting a large tip without recognition. Outside the café Stephen said, 'Sunday then.' But his wife was already walking away and did not hear.

That night he had the wet dream. The dream itself concerned the café, the girl and the coffee machine. It ended in sudden and intense pleasure, but for the moment the details were beyond recall. He got out of the bath hot and dizzy, on the edge, he thought, of an hallucination. Balanced on the side of the bath, he waited for it to wear off, a certain warping of the space between objects. He dressed and went outside, into the small garden of dying trees he shared with other residents in the square. It was seven o'clock. Already Drake, self-appointed custodian of the garden, was down on his knees by one of the benches. Paint-scraper in one hand, a bottle of colourless liquid in the other.

'Pigeon crap,' Drake barked at Stephen. 'Pigeons crap and no one can sit down. No one.' Stephen stood behind the old man, his hands deep in his pockets, and watched him work at the grey and white stains. He felt comforted. Round the edge of the garden ran a narrow path worn to a trough by the daily traffic of dog walkers, writers with blocks and married couples in crisis.

Walking there now Stephen thought, as he often did, of Miranda his daughter. On Sunday she would be fourteen, today he should find her a present. Two months ago she sent him a letter. 'Dear Daddy, are you looking after yourself? Can I have twenty-five pounds please to buy a record-player? With all my love, Miranda.' He replied by return post and regretted it the instant the letter left his hands. 'Dear Miranda, I *am* looking after myself, but not sufficiently to comply with ... etc.' In effect it was his wife he had addressed. At the sorting office he spoke to a sympathetic official who led him away by the elbow. You wish to retrieve a letter? This way please. They passed through a glass door and stepped out on to a small balcony. The kindly official indicated with a sweep of his hand the spectacular view, two acres of men, women, machinery and moving conveyor belts. Now where would you like us to start?

Returning to his point of departure for the third time he noticed that Drake was gone. The bench was spotless and smelling of spirit. He sat down. He had sent Miranda thirty pounds, three new ten-pound notes in a registered letter. He regretted that too. The extra five so clearly spelled out his guilt. He spent two days over a letter to her, fumbling, with reference to nothing in particular, maudlin. 'Dear Miranda, I heard some pop music on the radio the other day and I couldn't help wondering at the words which ... ' To such a letter he could conceive of no reply. But it came about ten days later. 'Dear Daddy, thanks for the money. I bought a Musivox Junior the same as my friend Charmian. With all my love, Miranda. PS It's got two speakers.'

Back indoors he made coffee, took it into his study and fell into the mild trance which allowed him to work three and a half hours without a break. He reviewed a pamphlet on Victorian attitudes to menstruation, he completed another three pages of a short story he was writing, he wrote a little in his random journal. He typed, 'nocturnal emission like an old man's last gasp' and crossed it out. From a drawer he took a thick ledger and entered in the credit column 'Review ... 1500 words. Short story ... 1020 words. Journal ... 60 words'. Taking a red biro from a box marked 'pens' he ruled off the day, closed the book and returned it to its drawer. He replaced the dust-cover on his typewriter, returned the telephone to its cradle, gathered up the coffee things on to a tray and carried them out, locking the study door behind him, thus terminating the morning's rite, unchanged for twenty-three years.

He moved quickly up Oxford Street gathering presents for his daughter's birthday. He bought a pair of jeans, a pair of coloured canvas running shoes suggestive of the Stars and Stripes. He bought three coloured T-shirts with funny slogans ... It's Raining In My Heart, Still a Virgin, and Ohio State University. He bought a pomander and a game of dice from a woman in the street and a necklace of plastic beads. He bought a book about women heroes, a game with mirrors, a record token for £5, a silk scarf and a glass pony. The silk scarf putting him in mind of underwear, he returned to the shop determined.

The erotic, pastel hush of the lingerie floor aroused in him a sense of taboo, he longed to lie down somewhere. He hesitated at the entrance to the department then turned back. He bought a bottle of cologne on another floor and came home in a mood of gloomy excitement. He arranged his presents on the kitchen table and surveyed them with loathing, their sickly excess and condescension. For several minutes he stood in front of the kitchen table staring at each object in turn, trying to relive the certainty with which he had bought it. The record token he put on one side, the rest he swept into a carrier bag and threw it into the cupboard in the hallway. Then he took off his shoes and socks, lay down on his unmade bed, examined with his finger the colourless stain that had hardened on the sheet, and then slept till it was dark.

Naked from the waist Miranda Cooke lay across her bed, arms spread, face buried deep in the pillow, and the pillow buried deep under her yellow hair. From a chair by the bed a pink transistor radio played methodically through the top twenty. The late afternoon sun shone through closed curtains and cast the room in the cerulean green of a tropical aquarium. Little Charmian sat astride Miranda's buttocks, tiny Charmian, Miranda's friend, plied her finger nails backwards and forwards across Miranda's pale unblemished back.

Charmian too was naked, and time seemed to stand still. Ranged along the mirror of the dressing table, their feet concealed by cosmetic jars and tubes, their hands raised in perpetual surprise, sat the discarded dolls of Miranda's childhood. Chairmian's caresses slowed to nothing, her hands came to rest in the small of her friend's back. She stared at the wall in front of her, swaying abstractedly. Listening.

> ... They're all locked in the nursery,
> They got earphone heads, they got dirty necks,
> They're so twentieth century.

'I didn't know *that* was in,' she said. Miranda twisted her head and spoke from under her hair.

'It's come back,' she explained. 'The Rolling Stones used to sing it.'

Don'cha think there's a place for you
In between the sheets?

When it was over Miranda spoke peevishly over the
dj's hysterical routine. 'You've stopped. Why have you
stopped?'
'I've been doing it for ages.'
'You said half an hour for my birthday. You promised.'
Charmian began again. Miranda, sighing as one who
only receives her due, sank her mouth into the pillow.
Outside the room the traffic droned soothingly, the pitch
of an ambulance siren rose and fell, a bird began to sing,
broke off, started again, a bell rang somewhere downstairs
and later a voice called out, over and over again, another
siren passed, this time more distant ... it was all so remote
from the aquatic gloom where time had stopped, where
Charmian gently drew her nails across her friend's back
for her birthday. The voice reached them again. Miranda
stirred and said, 'I think that's my mum calling me. My
dad must've come.'
When he rang the front door bell, this house where he
had lived sixteen years, Stephen assumed his daughter
would answer. She usually did. But it was his wife. She
had the advantage of three concrete steps and she glared
down at him, waiting for him to speak. He had nothing
ready for her.
'Is ... is Miranda there?' he said finally. I'm a little
late,' he added, and taking his chance, advanced up the
steps. At the very last moment she stepped aside and
opened the door wider.
'She's upstairs,' she said tonelessly as Stephen tried to
squeeze by without touching her. 'We'll go in the big
room.' Stephen followed her into the comfortable, un-
changing room, lined from floor to ceiling with books he
had left behind. In one corner, under its canvas cover, was

his grand piano. Stephen ran his hand along its curving edge. Indicating the books he said, 'I must take all these off your hands.'

'In your own good time,' she said as she poured sherry for him. 'There's no hurry.' Stephen sat down at the piano and lifted the cover.

'Do either of you play it now?' She crossed the room with his glass and stood behind him.

'I never have the time. And Miranda isn't interested now.' He spread his hands over a soft, spacious chord, sustained it with the pedal and listened to it die away.

'Still in tune then?'

'Yes.' He played more chords, he began to improvise a melody, almost a melody. He could happily forget what he had come for and be left alone to play for an hour or so, his piano.

'I haven't played for over a year,' he said by way of explanation. His wife was over by the door now about to call out to Miranda, and she had to snatch back her breath to say,

'Really? It sounds fine to me. Miranda,' she called, 'Miranda, Miranda,' rising and falling on three notes, the third note higher than the first, and trailing away in-quisitively. Stephen played the three-note tune back, and his wife broke off abruptly. She looked sharply in his direction. 'Very clever.'

'You know you have a musical voice,' said Stephen without irony. She advanced farther into the room.

'Are you still intending to ask Miranda to stay with you?' Stephen closed the piano and resigned himself to hostilities.

'Have you been working on her then?' She folded her arms.

'She won't go with you. Not alone anyway.'

'There isn't room in the flat for you as well.'

'And thank God there isn't.' Stephen stood up and raised his hand like an Indian chief.

'Let's not,' he said. 'Let's not.' She nodded and returned to the door and called out to their daughter in a steady tone, immune to imitation. Then she said quietly, 'I'm talking about Charmian. Miranda's friend.'

'What's she like?'

She hesitated. 'She's upstairs. You'll see her.'

'Ah ... '

They sat in silence. From upstairs Stephen heard giggling, the familiar, distant hiss of the plumbing, a bedroom door opening and closing. From his shelves he picked out a book about dreams and thumbed through. He was aware of his wife leaving the room, but he did not look up. The setting afternoon sun lit the room. 'An emission during a dream indicates the sexual nature of the whole dream, however obscure and unlikely the contents are. Dreams culminating in emission may reveal the object of the dreamer's desire as well as his inner conflicts. An orgasm cannot lie.'

'Hello, Daddy,' said Miranda. 'This is Charmian, my friend.' The light was in his eyes and at first he thought they held hands, like mother and child side by side before him, illuminated from behind by the orange dying sun, waiting to be greeted. Their recent laughter seemed concealed in their silence. Stephen stood up and embraced his daughter. She felt different to the touch, stronger perhaps. She smelt unfamiliar, she had a private life at last, accountable to no one. Her bare arms were very warm.

'Happy birthday,' Stephen said, closing his eyes as he squeezed her and preparing to greet the minute figure at her side. He stepped back smiling and virtually knelt before her on the carpet to shake hands, this doll-like figurine who stood no more than 3 foot 6 at his daughter's side, whose wooden, oversized face smiled steadily back at him.

'I've read one of your books,' was her calm first remark. Stephen sat back in his chair. The two girls still stood before him as though they wished to be described and compared. Miranda's T-shirt did not reach her waist by several inches and her growing breasts lifted the edge of the shirt clear of her belly. Her hand rested on her friend's shoulder protectively.

'Really?' said Stephen after some pause. 'Which one?'

'The one about evolution.'

'Ah ... ' Stephen took from his pocket the envelope containing the record token and gave it to Miranda. 'It's not much,' he said, remembering the bag full of gifts. Miranda retired to a chair to open her envelope. The dwarf however remained standing in front of him, regarding him fixedly. She fingered the hem of her child's dress.

'Miranda told me a lot about you,' she said politely. Miranda looked up and giggled.

'No I didn't,' she protested. Charmian went on.

'She's very proud of you.' Miranda blushed. Stephen wondered at Charmian's age.

'I haven't given her much reason to be,' he found himself saying, and gestured at the room to indicate the nature of his domestic situation. The tiny girl gazed patiently into his eyes and he felt for a moment poised on the edge of total confession. I never satisfied my wife in marriage, you see. Her orgasms terrified me. Miranda had discovered her present. With a little cry she left her chair, cradled his head between her hands and stooping down kissed his ear.

'Thank you,' she murmured hotly and loudly, 'thank you, thank you.' Charmian took a couple of paces nearer till she was almost standing between his open knees. Miranda settled on the arm of his chair. It grew darker.

He felt the warmth of Miranda's body on his neck. She slipped down a little farther and rested her head on his shoulder. Charmian stirred. Miranda said, 'I'm glad you came,' and drew her knees up to make herself smaller. From outside Stephen heard his wife moving from one room to another. He lifted his arm round his daughter's shoulder, careful not to touch her breasts, and hugged her to him.

'Are you coming to stay with me when the holidays begin?'

'Charmian too ... ' She spoke childishly, but her words were delicately pitched between inquiry and stipulation.

'Charmian too,' Stephen agreed. 'If she wants to.' Charmian let her gaze drop and said demurely, 'Thank you.'

During the following week Stephen made preparations. He swept the floor of his only spare room, he cleaned the windows there and hung new curtains. He hired a television. In the mornings he worked with customary numbness and entered his achievements in the ledger book. He brought himself at last to set out what he could remember of his dream. The details seemed to be accumulating satisfactorily. His wife was in the café. It was for her that he was buying coffee. A young girl took a cup and held it to the machine. But now *he* was the machine, now *he* filled the cup. This sequence, laid out neatly, cryptically in his journal, worried him less now. It had, as far as he was concerned, a certain literary potential. It needed fleshing out, and since he could remember no more he would have to invent the rest. He thought of Charmian, of how small she was, and he examined carefully the chairs ranged round the dining-room table. She was small enough for a baby's high chair. In a department store he carefully chose two cushions. The impulse to buy the girls presents he distrusted and resisted. But still he wanted to

do things for them. What could he do? He raked out gobs
of ancient filth from under the kitchen sink, poured dead
flies and spiders from the lamp fixtures, boiled fetid dish-
cloths; he bought a toilet brush and scrubbed the crusty
bowl. Things they would never notice. Had he really
become such an old fool? He spoke to his wife on the
phone.

'You never mentioned Charmian before.'

'No,' she agreed. 'It's a fairly recent thing.'

'Well ... ' he struggled, 'how do you feel about it?'

'It's fine by me,' she said, very relaxed. 'They're good
friends.' She was trying him out, he thought. She hated
him for his fearfulness, his passivity and for all the wasted
hours between the sheets. It took her many years of
marriage to say so. The experimentation in his writing, the
lack of it in his life. She hated him. And now she had a
lover, a vigorous lover. And still he wanted to say, Is it
right, our lovely daughter with a friend who belongs by
rights in a circus or silk-hung brothel serving tea? Our
flaxen-haired, perfectly formed daughter, our tender bud,
is it not perverse?

'Expect them Thursday evening,' said his wife by way
of goodbye.

When Stephen answered the door he saw only Charmian
at first, and then he made out Miranda outside the tight
circle of light from the hall, struggling with both sets of
luggage. Charmian stood with her hands on her hips, her
heavy head tipped slightly to one side. Without greeting
she said, 'We had to take a taxi and he's downstairs
waiting.'

Stephen kissed his daughter, helped her in with the cases
and went downstairs to pay the taxi. When he returned, a
little out of breath from the two flights of stairs, the front
door of his flat was closed. He knocked and had to wait. It

was Charmian who opened the door and stood in his path.

'You can't come in,' she said solemnly. 'You'll have to come back later,' and she made as if to close the door. Laughing in his nasal, unconvincing way, Stephen lunged forwards, caught her under her arms and scooped her into the air. At the same time he stepped into the flat and closed the door behind him with his foot. He meant to lift her high in the air like a child, but she was heavy, heavy like an adult, and her feet trailed a few inches above the ground, it was all he could manage. She thumped his hand with her fists and shouted.

'Put me ... ' Her last word was cut off by the crash of the door. Stephen released her instantly. ' ... down,' she said softly. They stood in the bright hallway, both a little out of breath. For the first time he saw Charmian's face clearly. Her head was bullet shaped and ponderous, her lower lip curled permanently outwards and she had the beginnings of a double chin. Her nose was squat and she had the faint downy greyness of a moustache. Her neck was thick and bullish. Her eyes were large and calm, set far apart, brown like a dog's. She was not ugly, not with these eyes. Miranda was at the far end of the long hall. She wore ready-faded jeans and a yellow shirt. Her hair was in plaits and tied at the end with a scrap of blue denim. She came and stood by her friend's side.

'Charmian doesn't like being lifted about,' she explained. Stephen guided them towards his sitting room.

'I'm sorry,' he said to Charmian and laid his hand on her shoulder for an instant. 'I didn't know that.'

'I was only joking when I came to the door,' she said evenly.

'Yes of course,' Stephen said hurriedly. 'I didn't think anything else.'

During dinner, which Stephen had bought ready-cooked from a local Italian restaurant, the girls talked to him about their school. He allowed them a little wine and they giggled a lot and clutched at each other when they fell about. They prompted each other through a story about their head master who looked up girls' skirts. He remembered some anecdotes of his own time at school, or perhaps they were other people's time, but he told them well and they laughed delightedly. They became very excited. They pleaded for more wine. He told them one glass was enough.

Charmian and Miranda said they wanted to do the dishes. Stephen sprawled in an armchair with a large brandy, soothed by the blur of their voices and the homely clatter of dishes. This was where he lived, this was his home. Miranda brought him coffee. She sat it down on the table with the mock deference of a waitress.

'Coffee, sir?' she said. Stephen moved over in his chair and she sat in close beside him. She moved easily between woman and child. She drew her legs up like before and pressed herself against her large shaggy father. She had unloosened her plaits and her hair spread across Stephen's chest, golden in the electric light.

'Have you found a boyfriend at school?' he asked.

She shook her head and kept it pressed against his shoulder.

'Can't find a boyfriend, eh?' Stephen insisted. She sat up suddenly and lifted her hair clear of her face.

'There are loads of boys,' she said angrily, 'loads of them, but they're so *stupid*, they're such show-offs.' Never before had the resemblance between his wife and daughter seemed so strong. She glared at him. She included him with the boys at school. 'They're always doing things.'

'What sort of thing?' She shook her head impatiently.

'I don't know ... the way they comb their hair and bend their knees.'

'Bend their knees?'

'Yes. When they think you're watching them. They stand in front of our window and pretend they're combing their hair when they're just looking in at us, showing off. Like this.' She sprang out of the chair and crouched in the centre of the room in front of an imaginary mirror, bent low like a singer over a microphone, her head tilted grotesquely, combing with long, elaborate strokes; she stepped back, preened and then combed again. It was a furious imitation. Charmian was watching it too. She stood in the doorway with coffee in each hand.

'What about you, Charmian,' Stephen said carelessly, 'do you have a boyfriend?' Charmian set the coffee cups down and said, 'Of course I don't,' and then looked up and smiled at them both with the tolerance of a wise old woman.

Later on he showed them their bedroom.

'There's only one bed,' he told them. 'I thought you wouldn't mind sharing it.' It was an enormous bed, seven foot by seven, one of the few large objects he had brought with him from his marriage. The sheets were deep red and very old, from a time when all sheets were white. He did not care to sleep between them now, they had been a wedding present. Charmian lay across the bed, she hardly took up more room than one of the pillows. Stephen said goodnight. Miranda followed him into the hall, stood on tiptoe to kiss him on the cheek.

'*You're* not a show-off,' she whispered and clung to him. Stephen stood perfectly still. 'I wish you'd come home,' she said. He kissed the top of her head.

'This is home,' he said. 'You've got two homes now.' He broke her hold and led her back to the entrance of the bedroom. He squeezed her hand. 'See you in the morning,' he murmured, left her there and hurried into his study. He sat down, horrified at his erection, elated. Ten minutes passed. He thought he should be sombre, analytical, this was a serious matter. But he wanted to sing, he wanted to play his piano, he wanted to go for a walk. He did none of those things. He sat still, staring ahead, thinking of nothing in particular, and waited for the chill of excitement to leave his belly.

When it did he went to bed. He slept badly. For many hours he was tormented by the thought that he was still awake. He awoke completely from fragmentary, dreams into total darkness. It seemed to him then that for some time he had been hearing a sound. He could not remember what the sound was, only that he had not liked it. It was silent now, the darkness hissed about his ears. He wanted to piss, and for a moment he was afraid to leave his bed. The certainty of his own death came to him now as it occasionally did, as a sick revelation, not the dread of dying, but of dying now, 3.15 am, lying still with the sheet drawn up round his neck and wanting, like all mortal animals, to urinate. He turned the light on and went into the bathroom. His cock was small in his hands, nut brown and wrinkled by the cold, or perhaps the fear. He felt sorry for it. As he pissed his stream split in two. He pulled his foreskin a little and the streams converged. He felt sorry for himself. He stepped back into the hallway, and as he closed the bathroom door behind him and cut off the rumble of the cistern he heard that sound again, the sound he had listened to in his sleep. A sound so forgotten, so utterly familiar that only now as he advanced very cautiously along the hallway did he know it to be the background for all other sounds, the frame of all anxieties. The sound of his wife in, or approaching, orgasm. He stopped several yards short of the girls' bedroom. It was a low moan through the medium of a harsh, barking cough, it rose imperceptibly in pitch through fractions of a tone, then fell away at the end, down but not very far, still higher than the starting-point. He did not dare go nearer the door. He strained to listen. The end came and he heard the bed creak a little, and footsteps across the floor. He saw the door handle turn. Like a dreamer he asked no questions, he forgot his nakedness, he had no expectations.

Miranda screwed up her eyes in the brightness. Her yellow hair was loose. Her white cotton nightdress reached her ankles and its folds concealed the lines of her body. She could be any age. She hugged her arms round her body. Her father stood in front of her, very still, very massive, one foot in front of the other as though frozen mid-step, arms limp by his side, his naked black hairs, his wrinkled, nut-brown naked self. She could be a child or a woman, she could be any age. She took a little step forward.

'Daddy,' she moaned, 'I can't get to sleep.' She took his hand and he led her into the bedroom. Charmian lay curled up on the far side of the bed, her back to them. Was she awake, was she innocent? Stephen held back the bedclothes and Miranda climbed between the sheets. He tucked her in and sat on the edge of the bed. She arranged her hair.

'Sometimes I get frightened when I wake up in the middle of the night,' she told him.

'So do I,' he said and bent over and kissed her lightly on the lips.

'But there's nothing to be frightened of really, is there?'

'No,' he said, 'Nothing.' She settled herself deeper into the deep red sheets and gazed into his face.

'Tell me something though, tell me something to make me go to sleep.' He looked across at Charmian.

'Tomorrow you can look in the cupboard in the hall. There's a whole bag of presents in there.'

'For Charmian too?'

'Yes.' He studied her face by the light from the hall. He was beginning to feel the cold. 'I bought them for your birthday,' he added. But she was asleep and almost smiling, and in the pallor of her upturned throat he thought he saw from one bright morning in his childhood a field of dazzling white snow which he, a small boy of eight, had not dared scar with footprints.

To and Fro

❧❧

Now Leech pushes his legs out straight till they tremble with the effort, locks his fingers behind his head, cracks them at the joints, chuckles his deliberate, dirty chuckle at what he pretends to see in the middle distance and bats me gently behind the head with his elbow. Looks like it's over, what would you say?

Is it true? I lie in the dark. It is true, I think the old to and fro rocked her to sleep. The ancient to and fro had no end and the suspension came unnoticed like sleep itself. Rise and fall, rise and fall, rise and fall, between the fall and rise the perilous silent gap, the decision she makes to go on.

The sky a blank yellow-white, the canal odour reduced by distance to the smell of sweet ripe cherries, the melancholy of airliners turning in the stack and here in the office others cut up the day's papers, this is their work. Paste columns to index cards.

If I can lie in the dark I can see in the dark pale skin on the fragile ridge of cheekbone, it carves a dog-leg shape in the dark. The deep-set eyes are open and invisible. Through almost parted lips a point of light glints on saliva and tooth, the thick belt of hair blacker than the surrounding night. Sometimes I look at her and wonder who will die first, who will die first, you or me? The colossal weight of stillness, how many more hours?

Leech. I see Leech in this same corridor in frequent consultation with the Director. I see them, together they pace the long doorless corridor. The Director walks erect, his hands, deep in his pockets, jingle with gewgaws and Leech stoops subordinately, head twisted towards his superior's neck, his hands clasped behind his back, the fingers of one hand rolled around the wrist of the other to check scrupulously his own pulse. I see what the Director sees, our images combine — Leech and this man; twist the bright metal ring and they spring apart, one standing, one sitting, both posing.

Saliva glints on a point of tooth. Listen to her breathing, rhythmic soaring and plunging, deep sleep air, not her now. One animal need tracks another through the night, black-furred sleep smothered pleasure from a low branch, the old tree creaks, gone, memory, listen to her ... house smells sweet. The ancient, soft to and fro rocked her to sleep. Do you remember the small wood, the gnarled and stunted trees, the leafless branches and twigs fused to one canopy, what we found there? What we saw? Ah ... the tiny, patient heroism of being awake, the arctic hole bigger than the surrounding ice widens, too large to assume a shape, inclusive of the optical limits of sight. I lie in the dark and look in, I lie in it and gaze out, and from another room one of her children cries out in her sleep, A bear!

First here comes Leech, no first here am I towards the end on one morning, reclining, sipping, private, and Leech comes by, salutes me, claps me on the back a cordial, vicious blow between the shoulder blades below the neck. He stands at the tea urn, legs apart like a public urinator, the brown liquid dribbling into his cup and he saying do I remember (this) or (that) conversation. No, no. He approaches with his cup. No, no, I tell him, I remember nothing, I tell him as he settles on the long settee, as close to me as he can without actually ... becoming me. Ah, the bitter tang of a stranger's skin wrapped about to conceal the remoter fecal core. His right leg touches my left.

In the cold hour before dawn her children will climb into the bed, first one and then the other, sometimes one without the other, they drop between the spicy adult warmth, attach themselves to her sides like the starfish (remember the starfish clinging to its rock) and make faint liquid noises with their tongues. Outside in the street urgent footsteps approach and recede down the hill. I lie on the edge of the litter, Robinson Crusoe making his plans for stockades of finely sharpened stakes, guns that will fire themselves at the faintest tremor of an alien step, hopes his goats and dogs will procreate, will not find another such nest of tolerant creatures. When one of her daughters comes too early, in the dead of night she wakes and carries her back, returns and sleeps, her knees drawn up to her belly. Her house smells sweetly of sleeping children.

In the slow motion of one who feels the need to be watched, Leech unclips a pen from his breast pocket, examines it, replaces it, grips my extended arm as I reach for my book which slid to the floor at the moment of Leech's blow. A significant space by the door indicates the Director, the possibility of his arrival.

The colossal weight ... do you remember, sleeper, the small wood of gnarled stunted trees, the leafless branches and twigs fused to one canopy, a dark roof leaking light on to the pungent soil. We tiptoed on the absorbent vegetable silence, it made us whisper, drew our sibilants through hidden roots beneath our feet, a very old and private wood. Ahead of us brightness, the canopy had collapsed as though a heavy weight once crashed down from the sky. The bright semicircle, the trees' branches and twigs drooping to the ground in a brilliant cascade, and there lodged halfway up the torrent, picked white by the sun and stark against the dull grey wood were bones, white bones of a creature resting there, a flat, socketed skull, a long curving spine diminishing to the delicate point, and at its sides the meticulous heap of other bones, slender with bunch-fisted ends.

Leech's fingers have the tenacity of a chicken's claw. When I prise the fingers loose from my arm they curl back impersonally. Is this a lonely man? To whom, having touched his hand, I feel compelled to speak, as bright-eyed lovers on their backs under a sheet begin a conversation. I hold my own hands in my lap and watch motes fall across a slab of sunlight.

Sometimes I look at her and wonder who will die first ... face to face, wintering in the mess of down and patchwork, she places a hand over each of my ears, takes my head between her palms, regards me with thick, black eyes and pursed smile that does not show her teeth ... then I think, It's me, I shall die first, and you might live forever.

Leech sets down his cup (how brown he has made its rim), settles back, pushes his legs out straight till they tremble from the effort and watches with me motes falling across a slab of sunlight, and beyond that the ice hole, up, out, where I lie beside my sleeping lover, lie staring in, gazing back. I recognise the down and patchwork, the charm of the bed's wrought iron ... Leech sets down his cup, settles back, cracks his finger joints behind his head which he moves to indicate his intention to move, an awareness of the empty space by the door, a wish to be accompanied on the way.

A voice breaks the stillness, a brilliant red flower dropped on the snow, one of her daughters calls out in a dream, A bear! the sound indistinct from its sense. Silence, and then again, A bear, softer this time, with a falling tone of disappointment ... now, a silence dramatic for its absence of the succinct voice ... now imperceptibly ... now, habitual silence, no expectations, the weight of stillness, the luminous after-image of bears in fading orange. I watch them go and lie waiting beside my sleeping friend, turn my head on the pillow and look into her open eyes.

I rise at last and follow Leech across the empty room and along the doorless corridor where I have seen him in frequent consultation, pacing, erect or stooping. The Director and his subordinate, we cannot be told apart from those we fear ... I draw level with Leech and he is feeling the material of his suit, finger and thumb rotate either side of his lapel, the motion slowing to nothing as he considers his words which are, What do you think of it, my suit? accompanied by the faintest smile. We come to a halt in the corridor, face to face, below us our stunted reflections in the polished floor. We see each other's but not our own.

The thick belt of hair is blacker than the surrounding night, and pale skin on the fragile ridge of cheekbone carves a dog-leg shape in the dark ... Was that you? she murmurs, Or the children? Some faint movement where her eyes are say they are closed. The rhythm of her breathing strengthens, it is the impending automation of a sleeping body. It was nothing, it was a dream, a voice in the dark like a red flower on the snow ... she falls backwards, she drifts to the bottom of a deep well and looking up can watch the receding circle of light, of sky broken by the silhouette of my watching head and shoulders far away. She drifts down, her words drift up, passing her on the way and reach me muted by echoes. She calls, Come inside me while I fall asleep, come inside ...

With a similar manoeuvre of finger and thumb I reach out and touch the lapel and then touch my own, the familiar feel of each material, the body warmth they transmit ... the smell of sweet ripe cherries, the melancholy of airliners turning in the stack; this is the work, we cannot be told apart by those we fear. Leech grips my extended arm and shakes it. Open your eyes, open your eyes. You'll see it's not like yours at all. Here the lapels are wider, the jacket has two slits behind at my request and while they are the same shade of blue, mine has little flecks of white and the total effect is lighter. At the sound of footsteps far behind us we continue on our way.

Asleep and so moist? The synaesthesia of the ancient to and fro, the salt water and spice warehouses, a rise beyond which the contours smooth and roll and dip against the skyline like a giant tree hingeing on the sky, a tongue of flesh. I kiss and suck where her daughters sucked. Come away, she said, leave it alone. The white bones of some creature I wanted to approach and touch, the flat-socketed skull, the long curving spine diminishing to the delicate point ... Leave it alone, she said when I put out my arm. No mistaking the terror in those words, she said it was a nightmare and cluched our picnic to her —when we embraced, a bottle rattled against a tin. Holding hands we ran through the wood and out across the slopes, around the knots of gorse, the big valley below us, the good big clouds, the wood a flat scar on the dull green.

Yes, it is the Director's habit to advance several feet into the room and pause to survey the activities of his subordinates. But for a tightening in the air (the very space the air inhabits compresses) nothing changes, everyone looks, no one looks up ... The Director's look is sunk in fat bound by wonderful translucent skin, it has accumulated on the ridge of his cheekbone and now, like a glacier, seeps down into the hollow of his eye. The sunken authoritative eye sweeps the room, desk, faces, the open window, and fixes like a sluggish spinning bottle on me ... Ah Leech, he says.

In her house it smells sweetly of sleeping children, of cats drying in the warmth, of dust warming in the valves of an old radio – is this the news, fewer injured, more dead? How can I be sure the earth is turning towards the morning? In the morning I'll tell her across the empty cups and stains, more memory than dream, I claim waking status in my dreams. Nothing exaggerated but fine points of physical disgust and those exaggerated only appropriately, and all seen through, so I shall claim, a hole so big there was no ice to surround it.

It is tranquil here at the trestle table by the window. This is the work, not happy, not unhappy, sifting through the returned cuttings. This is the work, finding the categories appropriate to the filing system. The sky a blank yellow-white, the canal odour reduced by distance to the smell of sweet ripe cherries, the melancholy of airliners in the stack and elsewhere in the office others cut up the day's papers, paste columns to index cards; pollution/air, pollution/noise, pollution/water, the genteel sound of scissors, the shuffle of glue on pots, a hand pushing open the door. The Director advances several feet into the room and pauses to survey the activity of his subordinates.

I will tell her ... she sighs and stirs, sweeps her unbrushed hair clear of her watery eyes, goes to rise but remains sitting, cups her hands around a jug – a junk shop present to herself. In her eyes the window makes small bright squares, under her eyes cusps of blue twin-moon her white face. She pushes her hair clear, sighs and stirs.

He is walking towards me. Ah Leech, he says as he comes. He calls me Leech. Ah Leech, there's something I want you to do for me. Something I do not hear, mesmerised where I sit by the mouth which forms itself round the syllables. Something I want you to do for me. At the casual, unworried moment he realises his mistake, Leech occurs from behind a bank of cabinets, effusively forgiving. The Director is briskly apologetic. As my colleague will confirm, says Leech, people are always confusing us, and so saying he rests his hand on my shoulder, forgiving me too. A very easy mistake, colleague, to allow yourself to be confused with Leech.

Listen to her breathing, rise and fall, rise and fall, between the rise and fall the perilous gap, the decision she makes to go on ... the weight of hours. I will tell her and avoid confusion. Her eyes will budge from left to right and back, study each of my eyes in turn, compare them for honesty or shift in intent, dip intermittently to my mouth and round and round to make a meaning of a face, and likewise my eyes in hers, round and round our eyes will dance and chase.

I sit wedged between the two standing men and the

Director repeats his instructions, impatiently leaves us, and when he reaches the door turns to look back and smiles indulgently. Yes! I have never seen him smile. I see what he sees—twins as posed for a formal photograph. One stands, his hand settled for ever on the shoulder of the other who sits; possibly a confusion, a trick of the lens, for if we turn this bright metal ring their images coalesce and there is only one. Name of? Hopeful and with good reason ... anxious.

To and fro is my clock, will make the earth turn, the dawn come, bring her daughters to her bed ... to and fro laughs at the stillness, to and fro drops her children between the spicy adult warmth, attaches them to her sides like starfish, do you remember ... the thrill of seeing what you are not intended to see, the great rock thrust across the wet, striated sand, the water's edge receding against its will to the horizon, and in the rock-thrust the hungry pools sucked and slopped and sucked. A fat black boulder hung across a pool and beneath it there it hung, and stretched its legs and arms, you saw it first, so orange, bright, beautiful, singular, its dripping white dots. It clung to the black rock it commanded, and how the water slapped it against its rock while far away the sea receded. The starfish did not threaten like the bones for being dead, it threatened for being so awake, like a child's shout in the dead of night.

The body warmth they transmit. Are we the same? Leech, are we? Leech stretches, answers, bats, pushes, pretends, consults, flatters, stoops, checks, poses, approaches, salutes, touches, examines, indicates, grips, murmurs, gazes, trembles, shakes, occurs, smiles, faintly, so very faintly, says, Open your ... the warmth? ... open your eyes, open your eyes.

Is it true? I lie in the dark ... it is true, I think it is over. She sleeps, there was no end, the suspension came unnoticed like sleep itself. Yes, the ancient to and fro rocked her to sleep, and in sleep she drew me to her side and placed her leg over mine. The dark grows blue and grey and I feel on my temple, beneath her breast, the ancient tread of her heart to and fro.

Psychopolis

❦❧

Mary worked in and part-owned a feminist bookstore in
Venice. I met her there lunchtime on my second day in
Los Angeles. That same evening we were lovers, and not
so long after that, friends. The following Friday I chained
her by the foot to my bed for the whole weekend. It was,
she explained to me, something she 'had to go into to
come out of'. I remember her extracting (later, in a
crowded bar) my solemn promise that I would not listen
if she demanded to be set free. Anxious to please my new
friend, I bought a fine chain and diminutive padlock.
With brass screws I secured a steel ring to the wooden
base of the bed and all was set. Within hours she was
insisting on her freedom, and though a little confused I got
out of bed, showered, dressed, put on my carpet slippers
and brought her a large frying-pan to urinate in. She tried
on a firm, sensible voice.

'Unlock this,' she said. 'I've had enough.' I admit she
frightened me. I poured myself a drink and hurried out
on to the balcony to watch the sun set. I was not at all
excited. I thought to myself, If I unlock the chain she will
despise me for being weak. If I keep her there she might
hate me, but at least I will have kept my promise. The
pale orange sun dipped into the haze, and I heard her
shout to me through the closed bedroom door. I closed
my eyes and concentrated on being blameless.

A friend of mine once had analysis with an elderly man,

a Freudian with a well-established practice in New York. On one occasion my friend spoke at length about his doubts concerning Freud's theories, their lack of scientific credibility, their cultural particularity and so on. When he had done the analyst smiled genially and replied, 'Look around you!' And indicated with his open palm the comfortable study, the rubber plant and the begonia rex, the book-lined walls and finally, with an inward movement of the wrist which both suggested candour and emphasised the lapels of his tasteful suit, said, 'Do you really think I would have got to where I am now if Freud was wrong?'

In the same manner I said to myself as I returned indoors (the sun now set and the bedroom silent), the bare truth of the matter is that I am keeping my promise.

All the same, I felt bored. I wandered from room to room turning on the lights, leaning in doorways and staring in at objects that already were familiar. I set up the music stand and took out my flute. I taught myself to play years ago and there are many errors, strengthened by habit, which I no longer have the will to correct. I do not press the keys as I should with the very tips of my fingers, and my fingers fly too high off the keys and so make it impossible to play fast passages with any facility. Furthermore my right wrist is not relaxed, and does not fall, as it should, at an easy right angle to the instrument. I do not hold my back straight when I play, instead I slouch over the music. My breathing is not controlled by the muscles of my stomach, I blow carelessly from the top of my throat. My embouchure is ill-formed and I rely too often on a syrupy vibrato. I lack the control to play any dynamics other than soft or loud. I have never bothered to teach myself the notes above top G. My musicianship is poor, and slightly unusual rhythms perplex me. Above all I have no ambition to play any other than the same half-dozen pieces and I make the same mistakes each time.

Several minutes into my first piece I thought of her listening from the bedroom and the phrase 'captive audience' came into my mind. While I played I devised ways in which these words could be inserted casually into a sentence to make a weak, light-hearted pun, the humour of which would somehow cause the situation to be elucidated. I put the flute down and walked towards the bedroom door. But before I had my sentence arranged, my hand, with a kind of insensible automation, had pushed the door open and I was standing in front of Mary. She sat on the edge of the bed brushing her hair, the chain decently obscured by blankets. In England a woman as articulate as Mary might have been regarded as an aggressor, but her manner was gentle. She was short and quite heavily built. Her face gave an impression of reds and blacks, deep red lips, black, black eyes, dusky apple-red cheeks and hair black and sleek like tar. Her grandmother was Indian.

'What do you want?' she said sharply and without interrupting the motion of her hand.

'Ah,' I said. 'Captive audience!'

'What?' When I did not repeat myself she told me that she wished to be left alone. I sat down on the bed and thought, If she asks me to set her free I'll do it instantly. But she said nothing. When she had finished with her hair she lay down with her hands clasped behind her head. I sat watching her, waiting. The idea of asking her if she wished to be set free seemed ludicrous, and simply setting her free without her permission was terrifying. I did not even know whether this was an ideological or psycho-sexual matter. I returned to my flute, this time carrying the music stand to the far end of the apartment and closing the intervening doors. I hoped she couldn't hear me.

On Sunday night, after more than twenty-four hours of unbroken silence between us, I set Mary free. As the lock sprang open I said, 'I've been in Los Angeles less than a week and already I feel a completely different person.'

Though partially true, the remark was designed to give pleasure. One hand resting on my shoulder, the other massaging her foot Mary said, 'It'll do that. It's a city at the end of cities.'

'It's sixty miles across!' I agreed.

'It's a thousand miles deep!' cried Mary wildly and threw her brown arms about my neck. She seemed to have found what she had hoped for.

But she was not inclined to explanations. Later on we ate out in a Mexican restaurant and I waited for her to mention her weekend in chains and when, finally, I began to ask her she interrupted with a question. 'Is it really true that England is in a state of total collapse?'

I said yes and spoke at length without believing what I was saying. The only experience I had of total collapse was a friend who killed himself. At first he only wanted to punish himself. He ate a little ground glass washed down with grapefruit juice. Then when the pains began he ran to the tube station, bought the cheapest ticket and threw himself under a train. The brand new Victoria line. What would that be like on a national scale? We walked back from the restaurant arm in arm without speaking. The air hot and damp around us, we kissed and clung to each other on the pavement beside her car.

'Same again next Friday?' I said wryly as she climbed in, but the words were cut by the slam of her door. Through the window she waved at me with her fingers and smiled. I didn't see her for quite a while.

I was staying in Santa Monica in a large, borrowed apartment over a hire shop which specialised in renting out items for party givers and, strangely, equipment for 'sickrooms'. One side of the shop was given over to wineglasses, cocktail shakers, spare easy chairs, a banqueting table and a portable discotheque, the other to wheel-chairs, tilting beds, tweezers and bedpans, bright tubular steel and coloured rubber hoses. During my stay I noticed a number of these stores throughout the city. The manager was immaculately dressed and initially intimidating in his friendliness. On our first meeting he told me he was 'only twenty-nine'. He was heavily built and wore one of those thick drooping moustaches grown throughout America and England by the ambitious young. On my first day he came up the stairs and introduced himself as George Malone and paid me a pleasant compliment. 'The British,' he said, 'make damn good invalid chairs. The very best.'

'That must be Rolls-Royce,' I said. Malone gripped my arm.

'Are you shitting me? Rolls-Royce make … '

'No, no,' I said nervously. 'A … a joke.' For a moment his face was immobilised, the mouth open and black, and I thought, He's going to hit me. But he laughed.

'Rolls-Royce! That's neat!' And the next time I saw him he indicated the sickroom side of his shop and called out after me, 'Wanna buy a Rolls?' Occasionally we drank together at lunchtime in a red-lit bar off Colorado Avenue where George had introduced me to the barman as 'a specialist in bizarre remarks'.

'What'll it be?' said the barman to me.

'Pig oil with a cherry,' I said, cordially hoping to live up to my reputation. But the barman scowled and turning to George spoke through a sigh.

'What'll it be?'

It was exhilarating, at least at first, to live in a city of narcissists. On my second or third day I followed George's directions and walked to the beach. It was noon. A million stark, primitive figurines lay scattered on the fine, pale, yellow sand till they were swallowed up, north and south, in a haze of heat and pollution. Nothing moved but the sluggish giant waves in the distance, and the silence was awesome. Near where I stood on the very edge of the beach were different kinds of parallel bars, empty and stark, their crude geometry marked by silence. Not even the sound of the waves reached me, no voices, the whole city lay dreaming. As I began walking towards the ocean there were soft murmurs nearby, and it was as if I overheard a sleep-talker. I saw a man move his hand, spreading his fingers more firmly against the sand to catch the sun. An icebox without its lid stood like a gravestone at the head of a prostrate woman. I peeped inside as I passed and saw empty beercans and a packet of orange cheese floating in water. Now that I was moving among them I noticed how far apart each solitary sunbather was. It seemed to take minutes to walk from one to another. A trick of perspective had made me think they were jammed together. I noticed too how beautiful the women were, their brown limbs spread like starfish; and how many healthy old men there were with gnarled muscular bodies. The spectacle of this common intent exhilarated me and for the first time in my life I too urgently wished to be brown-skinned, brown-faced, so that when I smiled my teeth would flash white. I took off my trousers and shirt, spread my towel and lay down on my back thinking, I shall be free, I shall change beyond all recognition. But within minutes I was hot and restless, I longed to open my eyes. I ran into the ocean and swam out to where a few people were treading water and waiting for an especially huge wave to dash them to the shore.

Returning from the beach one day I found pinned to my door a note from my friend Terence Latterly. 'Waiting for you,' it said, 'in the Doggie Diner across the street.' I had met Latterly years ago in England when he was researching a still uncompleted thesis on George Orwell, and it was not till I came to America that I realised how rare an American he was. Slender, extraordinarily pallid, fine black hair that curled, doe eyes like a Renaissance princess, long straight nose with narrow black slits for nostrils, Terence was unwholesomely beautiful. He was frequently approached by gays, and once, in Polk Street San Francisco, literally mobbed. He had a stammer, slight enough to be endearing to those endeared by such things, and he was intense in his friendships to the point of occasionally lapsing into impenetrable sulks about them. It took me some time to admit to myself I actually disliked Terence and by that time he was in my life and I accepted the fact. Like all compulsive monologuists he lacked curiosity about other people's minds, but his stories were good and he never told the same one twice. He regularly became infatuated with women whom he drove away with his labyrinthine awkwardness and consumptive zeal, and who provided fresh material for his monologues. Two or three times now quiet, lonely, protective girls had fallen hopelessly for Terence and his ways, but, tellingly, he was not interested. Terence cared for long-legged, tough-minded, independent women who were rapidly bored by Terence. He once told me he masturbated every day.

He was the Doggie Diner's only customer, bent morosely over an empty coffee cup, his chin propped in his palms.

'In England,' I told him, 'a dog's dinner means some kind of unpalatable mess.'

'Sit down then,' said Terence. 'We're in the right place. I've been so humiliated.'

'Sylvie?' I asked obligingly.

'Yes yes. Grotesquely humiliated.' This was nothing new. Terence dined out frequently on morbid accounts of blows dealt him by indifferent women. He had been in love with Sylvie for months now and had followed her here from San Francisco, which was where he first told me about her. She made a living setting up health food restaurants and then selling them, and as far as I knew, she was hardly aware of the existence of Terence.

'I should never've come to Los Angeles,' Terence was saying as the Doggie Diner waitress refilled his cup. 'It's OK for the British. You see everything here as a bizarre comedy of extremes, but that's because you're out of it. The truth is it's psychotic, totally psychotic.' Terence ran his fingers through his hair which looked lacquered and stiff, and stared out into the street. Wrapped in a constant, faint blue cloud, cars drifted by at twenty miles an hour, their drivers propped their tanned forearms on the window ledges, their car radios and stereos were on, they were all going home or to bars for happy hour.

After a suitable silence I said, 'Well ... ?'

From the day he arrives in Los Angeles Terence pleads with Sylvie over the phone to have a meal with him in a restaurant, and finally, wearily, she consents. Terence buys a new shirt, visits a hairdresser and spends an hour in the late afternoon in front of the mirror, staring at his face. He meets Sylvie in a bar, they drink bourbon. She is relaxed and friendly, and they talk easily of Californian politics, of which Terence knows next to nothing. Since Sylvie knows Los Angeles she chooses the restaurant. As they are leaving the bar she says, 'Shall we go in your car or mine?'

Terence, who has no car and cannot drive, says, 'Why not yours?'

By the end of the *hors d'oeuvres* they are starting in on their second bottle of wine and talking of books, and then of money, and then of books again. Lovely Sylvie leads Terence by the hand through half a dozen topics; she

smiles and Terence flushes with love and love's wildest
ambitions. He loves so hard he knows he will not be able
to resist declaring himself. He can feel it coming on, a mad
confession. The words tumble out, a declaration of love
worthy of the pages of Walter Scott, its main burden being
that there is nothing, absolutely nothing, in the world
Terence would not do for Sylvie. In fact, drunk, he
challenges her now to test his devotion. Touched by the
bourbon and wine, intrigued by this wan, *fin de siècle*
lunatic, Sylvie gazes warmly across the table and returns
his little squeeze to the hand. In the rarefied air between
them runs a charge of goodwill and daredevilry. Pro-
pelled by mere silence Terence repeats himself. There is
nothing, absolutely nothing, in the etc. Sylvie's gaze shifts
momentarily from Terence's face to the door of the
restaurant through which a well-to-do middle-aged
couple are now entering. She frowns, then smiles.

'Anything?' she says.

'Yes yes, anything.' Terence is solemn now, sensing the
real challenge in her question. Sylvie leans forward and
grips his forearm.

'You won't back out?'

'No, if it's humanly possible I'll do it.' Again Sylvie is
looking over at the couple who wait by the door to be
seated by the hostess, an energetic lady in a red soldier-
like uniform. Terence watches too. Sylvie tightens her
grip on his arm.

'I want you to urinate in your pants, now. Go on now!
Quick! Do it now before you have time to think about it.'

Terence is about to protest, but his own promises still
hang in the air, an accusing cloud. With drunken sway,
and with the sound of an electric bell ringing in his ears,
he urinates copiously, soaking his thighs, legs and backside
and sending a small, steady trickle to the floor.

'Have you done it?' says Sylvie.

'Yes,' says Terence, 'But why ... ?' Sylvie half-rises from her seat and waves prettily across the restaurant at the couple standing by the door.

'I want you to meet my parents,' she says. 'I've just seen them come in.' Terence remains seated for the introductions. He wonders if he can be smelled. There is nothing he will not say to dissuade this affable, greying couple from sitting down at their daughter's table. He talks desperately and without a break ('as if I was some kinda bore'), referring to Los Angeles as a 'shithole' and its inhabitants as 'greedy devourers of each other's privacy'. Terence hints at a recent prolonged mental illness from which he has hardly recovered, and he tells Sylvie's mother that all doctors, especially women doctors, are 'assholes' (arseholes). Sylvie says nothing. The father cocks an eyebrow at his wife and the couple wander off without farewell to their table on the far side of the room.

Terence appeared to have forgotten he was telling his story. He was cleaning his nails with the tooth of a comb. I said, 'Well, you can't stop there. *What happened?* What's the explanation for all this?' Around us the diner was filling up, but no one else was talking.

Terence said, 'I sat on a newspaper to keep her car seat from getting wet. We didn't speak much and she wouldn't come in when we got to my place. She told me earlier she didn't like her parents much. I guess she was just fooling around.' I wondered if Terence's story was invented or dreamed for it was the paradigm of all his rejections, the perfect formulation of his fears or, perhaps, of his profoundest desires.

'People here,' Terence said as we left the Doggie Diner, 'live so far from each other. Your neighbour is someone forty minutes' car ride away, and when you finally get together you're out to wreck each other with the frenzy of having been alone.'

Something about that remark appealed to me and I invited Terence up to my place to smoke a joint with me. We stood about on the pavement a few minutes while he tried to decide whether he wanted to or not. We looked across the street through the passing traffic and into the store where George was demonstrating the disco equipment to a black woman. Finally Terence shook his head and said that while he was in this part of town he would go and visit a girl he knew in Venice.

'Take some spare underwear,' I suggested.

'Yeah,' he called over his shoulder as he walked away. 'See you!'

There were long pointless days when I thought, Everywhere on earth is the same. Los Angeles, California, the whole of the United States seemed to me then a very fine and frail crust on the limitless, subterranean world of my own boredom. I could be anywhere, I could have saved myself the effort and the fare. I wished in fact I was nowhere, beyond the responsibility of place. I woke in the morning stultified by oversleep. Although I was neither hungry nor thirsty, I ate breakfast because I dared not be without the activity. I spent ten minutes cleaning my teeth knowing that when I finished I would have to choose to do something else. I returned to the kitchen, made more coffee and very carefully washed the dishes. Caffeine aided my growing panic. There were books in the living room that needed to be studied, there was writing that needed completion but the thought of it all made me flush hot with weariness and disgust. For that reason I tried not to think about it, I did not tempt myself. It hardly occurred to me to set foot inside the living room.

Instead I went to the bedroom and made the bed and took great care over the 'hospital corners'. Was I sick? I lay down on the bed and stared at the ceiling without a

thought in my head. Then I stood up and with my hands
in my pockets stared at the wall. Perhaps I should paint it
another colour, but of course I was only a temporary
resident. I remembered I was in a foreign city and hurried
to the balcony. Dull, white, box-shaped shops and houses,
parked cars, two lawn sprinklers, festoons of telephone
cable everywhere, one palm tree teetering against the sky,
the whole lit by a cruel white glow of a sun blotted out by
high cloud and pollution. It was as obvious and self-
explanatory to me as a row of suburban English bunga-
lows. What could I do about it? Go somewhere else? I
almost laughed out loud at the thought.

More to confirm my state of mind than change it, I
returned to the bedroom and grimly picked up my flute.
The piece I intended to play, dog-eared and stained, was
already on the music stand, Bach's Sonata No. 1 in A
minor. The lovely opening Andante, a series of lilting
arpeggios, requires a flawless breathing technique to make
sense of the phrasing, yet from the beginning I am snatch-
ing furtively at breaths like a supermarket shoplifter, and
the coherence of the piece becomes purely imaginary,
remembered from gramophone recordings and superimposed over the present. At bar fifteen, four and a half
bars into the Presto, I fumble over the octave leaps but I
press on, a dogged, failing athlete, to finish the first
movement short of breath and unable to hold the last note
its full length. Because I catch most of the right notes in the
right order, I regard the Allegro as my showpiece. I play
it with expressionless aggression. The Adagio, a sweet
thoughtful melody, illustrates to me every time I play it
how out of tune my notes are, some sharp, some flat, none
sweet, and the semi-demi quavers are always mis-timed.
And so to the two Minuets at the end which I play with
dry, rigid persistence, like a mechanical organ turned by
a monkey. This was my performance of Bach's Sonata,

unaltered now in its details for as long as I could remember.

I sat down on the edge of the bed and almost imme-diately stood up again. I went to the balcony to look once more at the foreign city. Out on one of the lawns a small girl picked up a smaller girl and staggered a few steps with her. More futility. I went inside and looked at the alarm clock in the bedroom. Eleven forty. Do something, quick! I stood by the clock listening to its tick. I went from room to room without really intending to, sometimes surprised to find that I was back in the kitchen again fiddling with the cracked plastic handle of the wall can-opener. I went into the living room and spent twenty minutes drumming with my fingers on the back of a book. Towards the middle of the afternoon I dialled the time and set the clock exactly. I sat on the lavatory a long time and decided then not to move till I had planned what to do next. I remained there over two hours, staring at my knees till they lost their meaning as limbs. I thought of cutting my fingernails, that would be a start. But I had no scissors! I commenced to prowl from room to room once more, and then, towards the middle of the evening, I fell asleep in an armchair, exhausted with myself.

George at least appeared to appreciate my playing. He came upstairs once, having heard me from the shop, and wanted to see my flute. He told me he had never actually held one in his hands before. He marvelled at the intricacy and precision of its levers and pads. He asked me to play a few notes so he could see how it was held, and then he wanted me to show him how he could make a note for himself. He peered at the music on the stand and said he thought it was 'brilliant' the way musicians could turn such a mess of lines and dots into sounds. The way com-posers could think up whole symphonies with dozens of different instruments going at once was totally beyond him. I said it was beyond me too.

'Music,' George said with a large gesture of his arm, 'is a sacred art.' Usually when I wasn't playing my flute I left it lying about collecting dust, assembled and ready to play. Now I found myself pulling it into its three sections and drying them carefully and laying each section down like a favourite doll, in the felt-lined case.

George lived out in Simi Valley on a recently reclaimed stretch of desert. He described his house as 'empty and smelling of fresh paint still'. He was separated from his wife and two weekends a month had his children over to stay, two boys aged seven and eight. Imperceptibly George became my host in Los Angeles. He had arrived here penniless from New York city when he was twenty-two. Now he made almost forty thousand dollars a year and felt responsible for the city and my experience in it. Sometimes after work George drove me for miles along the freeway in his new Volvo.

'I want you to get the feel of it, the insanity of its size.'

'What's that building?' I would say to him as we sped past an illuminated Third Reichian colossus mounted on a manicured green hill. George would glance out of his window.

'I dunno, a bank or temple or something.' We went to bars, bars for starlets, bars for 'intellectuals' where screen-writers drank, lesbian bars and a bar where the waiters, lithe, smooth-faced young men, dressed as Victorian serving-maids. We ate in a diner founded in 1947 which served only hamburgers and apple pie, a renowned and fashionable place where waiting customers stood like hungry ghosts at the backs of those seated.

We went to a club where singers and stand-up come-dians performed in the hope of being discovered. A thin girl with bright red hair and sequined T-shirt reached the end of her passionately murmured song on a sudden shrill, impossible top note. All conversation ceased. Someone, perhaps maliciously, dropped a glass. Halfway through, the note became a warbling vibrato and the singer collapsed on the stage in an abject curtsy, arms held stiffly in front of her, fists clenched. Then she sprang to her tiptoes and held her arms high above her head with the palms flat as if to forestall the sporadic and indifferent applause.

'They all want to be Barbara Streisand or Liza Minnelli,' George explained as he sucked a giant cocktail through a pink plastic straw. 'But no one's looking for that kind of stuff anymore.'

A man with stooped shoulders and wild curly hair shuffled on to the stage. He took the microphone out of its rest, held it close to his lips and said nothing. He seemed to be stuck for words. He wore a torn, muddied denim jacket over bare skin, his eyes were swollen almost to the point of closing and under the right there ran a long scratch which ended at the corner of his mouth and gave him the look of a partly made-up clown. His lower lip trembled and I thought he was going to weep. The hand that was not holding the microphone worried a coin and looking at that I noticed the stains down his jeans, yes, fresh wet vomit clung there. His lips parted but no sounds came out. The audience waited patiently. Somewhere at the back of the room a wine bottle was opened. When he spoke finally it was to his fingernails, a low, cracked murmur.

'I'm such a goddamn mess!'

The audience broke into fallabout laughter and cheering, which after a minute gave way to footstamping and rhythmic clapping. George and I, perhaps constrained by each other's company, smiled. The man reappeared by the microphone the moment the last clapping died away.

Now he spoke rapidly, his eyes still fixed on his fingers. Sometimes he glanced worriedly to the back of the room and we caught the flash of the whites of his eyes. He told us he had just broken up with his girl-friend, and how, as he was driving away from her house, he had started to weep, so much so that he could not see to drive and had to stop his car. He thought he might kill himself but first he wanted to say goodbye to *her*. He drove to a call box but it was out of order and this made him cry again. Here the audience, silent till now, laughed a little. He reached his girl-friend from a drug store. As soon as she picked up the phone and heard his voice she began to cry too. But she didn't want to see him. She told him, 'It's useless, there's nothing we can do.' He put the phone down and howled with grief. An assistant in the drug store told him to leave because he was upsetting the other customers. He walked along the street thinking about life and death, it started to rain, he popped some amyl nitrate, he tried to sell his watch. The audience was growing restless, a lot of people had stopped listening. He bummed fifty cents off a bum. Through his tears he thought he saw a woman aborting a foetus in the gutter and when he got closer he saw it was cardboard boxes and a lot of old rags. By now the man was talking over a steady drone of conversation. Waitresses with silver trays circulated the tables. Suddenly the speaker raised his hand and said, 'Well, see you,' and he was gone. A few people clapped but most did not notice him leave.

Not long before I was due to leave Los Angeles George invited me to spend Saturday evening at his house. I would be flying to New York late the following day. He wanted me to bring along a couple of friends to make a small farewell party, and he wanted me to bring along my flute.

'I really want to sit,' said George, 'in my own home with a glass of wine in my hand and hear you play that thing.' I phoned Mary first. We had been meeting intermittently since our weekend. Occasionally she had come and spent the afternoon at my apartment. She had another lover she more or less lived with, but she hardly mentioned him and it was never an issue between us. After agreeing to come, Mary wanted to know if Terence was going to be there. I had recounted to her Terence's adventure with Sylvie, and described my own ambivalent feelings about him. Terence had not returned to San Francisco as he had intended. He had met someone who had a friend 'in screen writing' and now he was waiting for an introduction. When I phoned him he responded with an unconvincing parody of Semitic peevishness. 'Five weeks in this town and I'm invited out already?' I decided to take seriously George's wish to hear me play the flute. I practised my scales and arpeggios, I worked hard at those places in the Sonata No. 1 where I always faltered and as I played I fantasised about Mary, George and Terence listening spellbound and a little drunk, and my heart raced.

Mary arrived in the early evening and before driving to pick up Terence we sat around on my balcony watching the sun and smoked a small joint. It had been on my mind before she came that we might be going to bed for one last time. But now that she was here and we were dressed for an evening elsewhere, it seemed more appropriate to talk. Mary asked me what I had been doing and I told her about the night club act. I was not sure whether to present the man as a performer with an act so clever it was not funny, or as someone who had come in off the street and taken over the stage.

'I've seen acts like that here,' said Mary. 'The idea, when it works, is to make your laughter stick in your throat. What was funny suddenly gets nasty.' I asked

Mary if she thought there was any truth in my man's story. She shook her head.

'Everyone here,' she said, gesturing towards the setting sun, 'has got some kind of act going like that.'

'You seem to say that with some pride,' I said as we stood up. She smiled and we held hands for an empty moment in which there came to me from nowhere a vivid image of the parallel bars on the beach; then we turned and went inside.

Terence was waiting for us on the pavement outside the house where he was staying. He wore a white suit and as we pulled up he was fixing a pink carnation into his lapel. Mary's car had only two doors. I had to get out to let Terence in, but through a combination of sly manoeuvring on his part and obtuse politeness on my own, I found myself introducing my two friends from the back seat. As we turned on to the freeway Terence began to ask Mary a series of polite, insistent questions and it was clear from where I sat, directly behind Mary, that as she was answering one question he was formulating the next, or falling over himself to agree with everything she said.

'Yes, yes,' he was saying, leaning forwards eagerly, clasping together his long, pale fingers, 'That's a really good way of putting it.' Such condescension, I thought, such ingratiation. Why does Mary put up with it? Mary said that she thought Los Angeles was the most exciting city in the USA. Before she had even finished Terence was outdoing her with extravagant praise.

'I thought you hated it,' I interjected sourly. But Terence was adjusting his seat belt and asking Mary another question. I sat back and stared out the window, attempting to control my irritation. A little later Mary was craning her neck trying to find me in her mirror.

'You're very quiet back there,' she said gaily. I fell into sudden, furious mimicry.

'That's a really good way of putting it, yes, yes.' Neither Terence nor Mary made any reply. My words hung over us as though they were being uttered over and over again. I opened my window. We arrived at George's house with twenty-five minutes of unbroken silence behind us.

The introductions over, the three of us held the centre of George's huge living room while he fixed our drinks at the bar. I held my flute case and music stand under my arm like weapons. Apart from the bar the only other furniture was two yellow, plastic sag chairs, very bright against the desert expanse of brown carpet. Sliding doors took up the length of one wall and gave on to a small back yard of sand and stones in the centre of which, set in concrete, stood one of those tree-like contraptions for drying clothes on. In the corner of the yard was a scrappy sagebrush plant, survivor of the real desert that was here a year ago. Terence, Mary and I addressed remarks to George and said nothing to each other.

'Well,' said George when the four of us stood looking at each other with drinks in our hands, 'Follow me and I'll show you the kids.' Obediently we padded behind George in single file along a narrow, thickly carpeted corridor. We peered through a bedroom doorway at two small boys in a bunk bed reading comics. They glanced at us without interest and went on reading.

Back in the living room I said, 'They're very subdued, George. What do you do, beat them up?' George took my question seriously and there followed a conversation about corporal punishment. George said he occasionally gave the boys a slap on the back of the legs if things got really out of hand. But it was not to hurt them, he said, so much as to show them he meant business. Mary said she was dead against striking children at all, and Terence, largely to cut a figure I thought, or perhaps to demonstrate to me that he could disagree with Mary, said that he thought a sound thrashing never did anyone any harm. Mary laughed, but George, who obviously was not taking to this faintly foppish, languid guest sprawled across his carpet, seemed ready to move into the attack. George worked hard. He kept his back straight even when he sat in the sag chair.

'You were thrashed when you were a kid?' he asked as he handed round the scotch.

Terence hesitated and said, 'Yes.' This surprised me. Terence's father died before he was born and he had grown up with his mother in Vermont.

'Your mother beat you?' I said before he had time to invent a swaggering bully of a father.

'Yes.'

'And you don't think it did you any harm?' said George. 'I don't believe it.'

Terence stretched his legs. 'No harm done at all.' He spoke through a yawn that might have been a fake. He gestured towards his pink carnation. 'After all, here I am.'

There was a moment's pause then George said, 'For example, you never had any problem making out with women?' I could not help smiling.

Terence sat up. 'Oh yes,' he said. 'Our English friend here will verify that.' By this Terence referred to my outburst in the car. But I said to George, 'Terence likes to tell funny stories about his own sexual failures.'

George leaned forwards to catch Terence's full attention. 'How can you be sure they're not caused by being thrashed by your mother?'

Terence spoke very quickly. I was not sure whether he was very excited or very angry. 'There will always be problems between men and women and everyone suffers in some way. I conceal less about myself than other people do. I guess you never had your backside tanned by your mother when you were a kid, but does that mean you never have any hang-ups with women? I mean, where's your wife ... ?'

Mary's interruption had the precision of a surgeon's knife.

'I was only ever hit once as a kid, by my father, and do you know why that was? I was twelve. We were all sitting round the table at suppertime, all the family, and I told everyone I was bleeding from between my legs. I put some blood on the end of my finger and held it up for them all to see. My father leaned across the table and slapped my face. He told me not to be dirty and sent me up to my room.'

George got up to fetch more ice for our glasses and muttered 'Simply grotesque' as he went. Terence stretched out on the floor, his eyes fixed on the ceiling like a dead man's. From the bedroom came the sound of the boys singing, or rather chanting, for the song was all on one note. I said to Mary something to the effect that between people who had just met, such a conversation could not have taken place in England.

'Is that a good thing do you think?' Mary asked.

Terence said, 'The English tell each other nothing.'

I said, 'Between telling nothing and telling everything there is very little to choose.'

'Did you hear the boys?' George said as he came back.

'We heard some kind of singing,' Mary told him. George was pouring more scotch and spooning ice into the glasses.

'That wasn't singing. That was praying. I've been teaching them the Lord's Prayer.' On the floor Terence groaned and George looked round sharply.

'I didn't know you were a Christian, George,' I said.

'Oh, well, you know ... ' George sank into his chair. There was a pause, as if all four of us were gathering our strength for another round of fragmentary dissent.

Mary was now in the second sag chair facing George. Terence lay like a low wall between them, and I sat cross-legged about a yard from Terence's feet. It was George who spoke first, across Terence to Mary.

'I've never been interested in church-going much but ... ' He trailed off, a little drunkenly, I thought. 'But I always wanted the boys to have as much of it as possible while they're young. They can reject it later, I guess. But at least for now they have a coherent set of values that are as good as any other, and they have this whole set of stories, really good stories, exotic stories, believable stories.'

No one spoke so George went on. 'They like the idea of God. And heaven and hell, and angels and the Devil. They talk about that stuff a whole lot and I'm never sure quite what it means to them. I guess it's a bit like Santa Claus, they believe it and they don't believe it. They like the business of praying, even if they do ask for the craziest things. Praying for them is a kind of extension of their ... their inner lives. They pray about what they want and what they're afraid of. They go to church every week, it's about the only thing Jean and I agree on.'

George addressed all this to Mary who nodded as he spoke and stared back at him solemnly. Terence had closed his eyes. Now that he had finished, George looked at each of us in turn, waiting to be challenged. We stirred. Terence lifted himself on to his elbow. No one spoke.

'I don't see it's going to hurt them, a bit of the old religion,' George reiterated.

Mary spoke into the ground. 'Well, I don't know. There's a lot of things you could object to in Christianity. And since you don't really believe in it yourself we should talk about that.'

'OK,' said George. 'Let's hear it.'

Mary spoke with deliberation at first. 'Well, for a start, the Bible is a book written by men, addressed to men and features a very male God who even looks like a man because he made man in his own image. That sounds pretty suspicious to me, a real male fantasy ... '

'Wait a minute,' said George.

'Next,' Mary went on, 'women come off pretty badly in Christianity. Through Original Sin they are held responsible for everything in the world since the Garden of Eden. Women are weak, unclean, condemned to bear children in pain as punishment for the failures of Eve, they are the temptresses who turn the minds of men away from God; as if women were more responsible for men's sexual feelings than the men themselves! Like Simone de Beauvoir says, women are always the "other", the real business is between a man in the sky and the men on the ground. In fact women only exist at all as a kind of divine afterthought, put together out of a spare rib to keep men company and iron their shirts, and the biggest favour they can do Christianity is not to get dirtied up with sex, stay chaste, and if they can manage to have a baby at the same time then they're measuring up to the Christian Church's ideal of womanhood – the Virgin Mary.' Now Mary was angry, she glared at George.

'Wait a minute,' he was saying, 'you can't impose all that Women's Lib stuff on to the societies of thousands of years ago. Christianity expressed itself through available ... '

At roughly the same time Terence said, 'Another objection to Christianity is that it leads to passive acceptance of social inequalities because the real rewards are in ... '

And Mary cut in across George in protest. 'Christianity has provided an ideology for sexism now, and capitalism ... '

'Are you a communist?' George demanded angrily,

although I was not sure who he was talking to. Terence was pressing on loudly with his own speech. I heard him mention the Crusades and the Inquisition.

'This has nothing to do with Christianity.' George was almost shouting. His face was flushed.

'More evil perpetrated in the name of Christ than ... this has nothing to do with ... to the persecution of women herbalists as witches ... Bullshit. It's irrelevant ... corruption, graft, propping up tyrants, accumulating wealth at the altars ... fertility goddess ... bullshit ... phallic worship ... look at Galileo ... this has nothing to ... ' I heard little else because now I was shouting my own piece about Christianity. It was impossible to stay quiet. George was jabbing his finger furiously in Terence's direction. Mary was leaning forwards trying to catch George by the sleeve and tell him something. The whisky bottle lay on its side empty, someone had upset the ice. For the first time in my life I found myself with urgent views on Christianity, on violence, on America, on everything, and I demanded priority before my thoughts slipped away.

' ... and starting to think objectively about this ... their pulpits to put down the workers and their strikes so ... objective? You mean male. All reality now is male rea ... always a violent God ... the great capitalist in the sky ... protective ideology of the dominant class denies the conflict between men and women ... bullshit, total bullshit ... '

Suddenly I heard another voice ringing in my ears. It was my own. I was talking into a brief, exhausted silence.

' ... driving across the States I saw this sign in Illinois along Interstate 70 which said, "God, Guts, Guns made America great. Let's keep all three." '

'Hah!' Mary and Terence exclaimed in triumph. George was on his feet, empty glass in hand.

'That's right,' he cried. 'That's right. You can put it

down but it's right. This country has a violent past, a lot of brave men died making ... '

'Men!' echoed Mary.

'All right, and a lot of brave women too. America was made with the gun. You can't get away from that.' George strode across the room to the bar in the corner and drew out something black from behind the bottles. 'I keep a gun here,' he said, holding the thing up for us to see.

'What for?' Mary asked.

'When you have kids you begin to have a very different attitude towards life and death. I never kept a gun before the kids were around. Now I think I'd shoot at anyone who threatened their existence.'

'Is it a real gun?' I said. George came back towards us with the gun in one hand and a fresh bottle of scotch in the other. 'Dead right it's a real gun!' It was very small and did not extend beyond George's open palm.

'Let me see that,' said Terence.

'It's loaded,' George warned as he handed it across. The gun appeared to have a soothing effect on us all. We no longer shouted, we spoke quietly in its presence. While Terence examined the gun George filled our glasses. As he sat down he reminded me of my promise to play the flute. There followed a bleary silence of a minute or two, broken only by George to tell us that after this drink we should eat dinner. Mary was far away in thought. She rotated her glass slowly between her finger and thumb. I lay back on my elbows and began to piece together the conversation we had just had. I was trying to remember how we arrived at this sudden silence.

Then Terence snapped the safety catch and levelled the gun at George's head.

'Raise your hands, Christian,' he said dully.

George did not move. He said, 'You oughtn't to fool around with a gun.' Terence tightened his grip. Of course he was fooling around, and yet I could see from where I was that his finger was curled about the trigger, and he was beginning to pull on it.

'Terence!' Mary whispered, and touched his back gently with her foot. Keeping his eyes on Terence, George sipped at his drink. Terence brought his other hand up to steady the gun which was aimed at the centre of George's face.

'Death to the gun owners.' Terence spoke without a trace of humour. I tried to say his name too, but hardly a sound left my throat. When I tried again I said something in my accelerating panic that was quite irrelevant.

'Who is it?' Terence pulled the trigger.

From that point on the evening collapsed into conventional, labyrinthine politenesses at which Americans, when they wish, quite outstrip the English. George was the only one to have seen Terence remove the bullets from the gun, and this united Mary and me in a state of mild but prolonged shock. We ate salad and cold cuts from plates balanced on our knees. George asked Terence about his Orwell thesis and the prospects of teaching jobs. Terence asked George about his business, fun party hire and sickroom requisites. Mary was questioned about her job in the feminist bookshop and she answered blandly, carefully avoiding any statement that might provoke discussion. Finally I was called on to elaborate on my travel plans, which I did in great and dull detail. I explained how I would be spending a week in Amsterdam before returning to London. This caused Terence and George to spend several minutes in praise of Amsterdam, although it was quite clear they had seen very different cities.

Then while the others drank coffee and yawned, I played my flute. I played my Bach sonata no worse than usual, perhaps a little more confidently for being drunk, but my mind ran on against the music. For I was weary of this music and of myself for playing it. As the notes transferred themselves from the page to the end of my fingers I thought, Am I still playing *this*? I still heard the echo of our raised voices, I saw the black gun in George's open palm, the comedian reappear from the darkness to take the microphone again, I saw myself many months ago setting out for San Francisco from Buffalo in a drive-away car, shouting out for joy over the roar of the wind through the open windows, It's me, I'm here, I'm coming ... where was the music for all this? Why wasn't I even looking for it? Why did I go on doing what I couldn't do, music from another time and civilisation, its certainty and perfection to me a pretence and a lie, as much as they had once been, or might still be, a truth to others. What should I look for? (I tooled through the second movement like a piano roll.) Something difficult and free. I thought of Terence's stories about himself, his game with the gun, Mary's experiment with herself, of myself in an empty moment drumming my fingers on the back of a book, the vast, fragmented city without a centre, without citizens, a city that existed only in the mind, a nexus of change or stagnation in individual lives. Picture and idea crashed drunkenly one after the other, discord battened to bar after bar of implied harmony and inexorable logic. For the pulse of one beat I glanced past the music at my friends where they sprawled on the floor. Then their after-image glowed briefly at me from the page of music. Possible, even likely, that the four of us would never see each other again, and against such commonplace tran-sience my music was inane in its rationality, paltry in its over-determination. Leave it to others, to professionals who could evoke the old days of its truth. To me it was nothing, now that I knew what I wanted. This genteel escapism ... crossword with its answers written in, I could play no more of it.

I broke off in the slow movement and looked up. I was about to say, 'I can't go on any more', but the three of them were on their feet clapping and smiling broadly at me. In parody of concert-goers George and Terence cupped their hands round their mouths and called out 'Bravo! Bravissimo!' Mary came forward, kissed me on the cheek and presented me with an imaginary bouquet. Overwhelmed by nostalgia for a country I had not yet left, I could do no more than put my feet together and make a bow, clasping the flowers to my chest.

Then Mary said, 'Let's go. I'm tired.'